Reuben Radding

TIMOTHY BRANDOFF received a BA from Goddard College and an MFA from New York University. His fellowships include the Sundance Institute's Screenwriters Lab, the Chesterfield Writer's Film Project, the Vermont Studio Center, and Yaddo. *Cornelius Sky* was a runner-up for the James Jones First Novel Fellowship. Brandoff operates a bus for the New York City Transit Authority.

CORNELIUS SKY

TIMOTHY BRANDOFF

Published by Akashic Books
©2019 Timothy Brandoff

Paperback ISBN: 978-1-61775-708-2
Library of Congress Control Number: 2018960629

Kaylie Jones Books
www.kayliejonesbooks.com

Akashic Books
Brooklyn, New York, USA
Ballydehob, Co. Cork, Ireland
Twitter: @AkashicBooks
Facebook: AkashicBooks
E-mail: info@akashicbooks.com
Website: www.akashicbooks.com

Also Available from Kaylie Jones Books

Starve the Vulture by Jason Carney
City Mouse by Stacey Lender
Death of a Rainmaker by Laurie Loewenstein
Unmentionables by Laurie Loewenstein
Like This Afternoon Forever by Jaime Manrique
Little Beasts by Matthew McGevna
Some Go Hungry by J. Patrick Redmond
The Year of Needy Girls by Patricia A. Smith
The Love Book by Nina Solomon
The Devil's Song by Lauren Stahl
All Waiting Is Long by Barbara J. Taylor
Sing in the Morning, Cry at Night by Barbara J. Taylor
Flying Jenny by Theasa Tuohy

From Oddities/Kaylie Jones Books

Angel of the Underground by David Andreas
Foamers by Justin Kassab
Strays by Justin Kassab
We Are All Crew by Bill Landauer
The Underdog Parade by Michael Mihaley
The Kaleidoscope Sisters by Ronnie K. Stephens

to Walis

Pity is the feeling which arrests the mind in the presence of whatsoever is grave and constant in human sufferings and unites it with the human sufferer. Terror is the feeling which arrests the mind in the presence of whatsoever is grave and constant in human sufferings and unites it with the secret cause.
—James Joyce, *Portrait of the Artist as a Young Man*

But we aren't a glum lot.
—Anonymous

CHAPTER ONE

"COPS AGAIN, THAT WHAT YOU WANT?" His wife was inside their apartment. Connie was outside. He was trying to get inside.

Key in hand, he attempted to enter for who knows how long. Intoxication sometimes induced a palsy, coordination slipped, while the minutes blended into weeks and months. A rest period seemed in order. He closed his eyes and paused for a moment, like an old draft horse on its legs.

"When are you going to get it?" she said.

Slowly, with drunken deliberation, Connie glided his face toward the lock's cylinder, and the recognition of its gleaming new luster hit him where he lived. "Son of a." He considered removing his jacket, to show somebody, anybody, he meant business, but he ultimately couldn't be bothered.

"The cops, you hear me—"

Connie started his assault, but if closely studied, it was an assault tapered by self-consciousness. He witnessed his own behavior, watched himself attack the door like a second-rate actor of the presentational variety.

"Off the fucking hinges," he roared, pounding the door with the flat of his hand. But just beneath the surface of the scene he thought, *Look at me go. What a fake, what a phony. I don't even want to be in there.*

"Scaring the kids, you bastard. On their way the cops, think I'm kidding?"

Connie let the door have it. "Off the hinges." He was still slapping and hammering with the flat of his hand when his neighbor Willie appeared with farce-like speed at the door of 3-B: tank top, gold cross, a stingy brim of straw at rest above a gentle Puerto Rican face.

"Connie, Con-Con, what's happening?" Willie's tone nothing if not a sweet attempt to distract and diffuse.

"Believe this, Will?"

The elevator's outer door pushed open onto the landing to the sound of crackling walkie-talkies. Two New York City Housing Authority cops, Walsh and Pacheco, poised to dispose of one more midnight shift, joined Connie in front of 3-A, hitting their marks just so.

"Cornelius," Walsh said.

"Déjà vu," Pacheco said.

Through his stupor Connie felt a degree of mortification, not for the cops' presence, which was in fact an encore performance, but the new element.

"Changed the lock," Connie said.

"That'll happen," Pacheco said.

"Could be she's trying to suggest something," said Walsh, who then lit a beautiful Marlboro, because there was still time, back here in the spring of 1974, to excuse yourself from the world for a brief respite, just you and your best friend nicotine.

Connie produced his own crumpled pack of Camels. Walsh helped him pinch one out and fire it up. Pacheco glanced away with mild disdain.

They wandered into the shiny red interior of the elevator and Pacheco pressed a button on the panel. The inner door and its square foot of scratched, mesh-wired window slid closed, and they descended through a silo of graffiti.

"Connie," Walsh said once outside the building, "let's talk a minute. What's this, the second—"

"Third," Pacheco said.

"She gets the restraint order, we got no choice. You, this routine of yours, waking everybody up."

"My home," Connie bellowed. "I live here."

"Not anymore," Pacheco said. "You're done. Get that through your head."

"Remember now, Con," Walsh said, "up to you."

In the predawn stillness Connie looked like he'd strayed from a parade of damaged people, the doorman's cap cocked at an angle on his head. He watched the cops return to their double-parked squad car on 25th Street.

The front yard with its playground artifacts looked so mournful at this hour. The miniature ceramic horse on a spring, its chipped paint and missing left eye. The tarnished aluminum sculpture of planet Saturn leaning precariously on its axis. Had he ever played with his kids in this yard? Did he love his children? He did love them, in a sentimental fashion, they were his boys, he loved them completely, his entire heart, he'd do anything, damn near very close to almost anything for them.

He found his way to a bench in the yard for forty-five minutes of something like sleep.

If a camera were pushed up close to Connie's face where dry white saliva collected at the corners of his mouth and tiny bubbles burst on his lips, it would find him mumbling indecipherably, a few phrases to unravel: —*shot his father's head clean off. The mother on all fours chasing chunks of skull across the chassis. Humpty Dumpty and such. Talk about a status reduction. Whereas my father put his head in the oven. Common style back then. Two dead fathers, two heads, one by suicide, one by*—

A bench slat's rivet grinding at his hip bullied him back to consciousness. He winced, uncurled himself, sat up. Night had broken. The birds in the trees of the projects cried out with abandonment. The overcast sky made sense, given his life, and Connie acknowledged the cloud cover as subtle tribute. Blue skies would have added to the campaign of mockery waged not just against him— he wasn't *that* solipsistic—but against all sentient beings, birds included. A tenderness welled up in Connie, his chest went soft, before he patted himself down for a smoke.

He looked up to the bedroom window of his children.

His older son, Arthur, a long-haired twelve-year-old fired by rage, stood framed by the building's burnished brick facade. The apparition pierced Connie's drunkenness and hangover, he felt the kid's hatred beaming down at him.

Or wait, could it be—not malice, but care and concern? Arthur kept vigil so Connie would not get rolled or otherwise beat to death, that was a thought.

It crossed his mind to offer a sign, some gesture, to let the boy know, *Yes, I see you, my son, you are recognized in my eyes*, when Arthur, as if sensing his father's intentions, reached in a sudden flurry for the window shade and vanished.

* * *

"Come in, sit down here." The windowless office, a cub-byhole off the lobby's back hall, a few paces down from Superintendent Walter Mezzola's apartment, contained wooden furniture that could have come from the Board of Education. A black rotary phone sat there like a prop, while a spindle captured work orders on its spike.

"Good morning, Walter," Connie said.

"Mr. Mezzola," Walter said. "Call me Mr. Mezzola."

"Even when it's just the two of us?"

"Make it easy on yourself, please, Con." Walter sniffed softly, once, twice. "Okay, an example: have you been drinking let's say?"

"Me?" Connie said. "What, like today already have I been drinking?"

"Because this—alcohol, drugs, whatnot, you name it—just cause, immediate dismissal, follow me now?"

Certain supers walked around in suits and ties and jobbed all the work out. Walter wore dungarees and flannel shirts and even suspenders when not too desper-ate to hide the joy that lived in his heart. He did all the paint jobs in the house, he was a first-rate painter. He had learned the trade in the army. "All in the prep," Walter would say, "the paint forget about." He was a perfectly decent electrician and plumber as well. He'd break a wall in a minute. "You cannot be afraid to break," he'd say. Carpentry, for unknown reasons, he stayed away from.

"Tell you go downstairs, clean out your locker—one two three, boom, you're gone, that's it. They call it im-mediate dismissal. Like you don't know what hit you, follow me?"

"I hear you, Walter."

"Hope so. I hate to fire a man."

"I know you do."

"How's that, that you know that?"

"Every other word."

"And why? Because it's true . . . Believe me, Con, clear blue sky. And you got, what, two write-ups already in your file. I lost count. Main point being, I don't want to fire you, last thing believe me that I want."

"I know you don't, Walter, you're a good man."

"You sure?" Walter said, and brought a match to a cigarillo. Walter smoked cigarillos and regular cigarettes and a variety of cigars—everything but a pipe. "Got another complaint and I don't want to say from who."

"Who?"

"That woman on eight."

"Saxton?"

"Pain in the ass. She, I don't know, something about you got fresh with somebody, a friend of hers, the elevator."

"I'm not perfect."

"Who is?" Walter said. "These people, they lose track."

"Tell me about it."

"Of the fact we are human beings."

"Glad you said it."

"Bottom line," Walter said, "try not to get too fresh, all right? I know you're a good person. People like you."

"Certain people."

"The right people," Walter said. "Couple those tenants on the board think you're sliced bread. Some kind of saint they got you pegged for. Ever since the big buff job! I'll get fired before you get fired."

"Nah, they appreciate you."

"They do?" Walter fished.

"Plus, I always put in a good word."

"That right?" Walter said, then the phone jangled just once. "Hello. Tell her I'll be there. Right. Now. No. Right, right," and he hung up. "So we straight?"

"Thank you, Walter."

"Let me get back to work."

Connie lit a cigarette and they sat there smoking and neither of them moved.

And with a sad smile Walter said, "It's true."

"What's that?"

Swiveling in his chair, Walter stopped and looked up into a corner of the room, fully exposing his throat to Connie, as if to say, Go ahead and cut it if you must, before declaring, "I will miss you when you're gone!" and Connie could not help but laugh.

Connie worked a swing shift. A few evenings in the front of the house, a few days in the back, and one midnight. He had a mental block regarding his schedule, which he kept on a piece of folded paper in his wallet, but the wallet had found its way into the active cycle of a washer and the schedule became torn and brittle, and it never crossed his mind to grab a pen and write it out again on a fresh page. Or maybe he honored the raggedy copy out of vague superstition. In any case, every time he doubted whether he had to be in, he removed the schedule from his wallet like a cautious archeologist on a dig. Forceps would have come in handy but fingertips did the trick.

He didn't mind the back of the house and in some ways preferred it. He mopped the stairwells top to bottom, collected the garbage on the service car, and at shift's end stacked it in a smart pile on the sidewalk outside the service entrance. He polished all the brass of the house, the elevator panels, canopy poles, and standpipes. He changed a bulb here and there and did some light dusting. He cased the mail into a wooden cart on wheels a legendary handyman named Horace had built for the house twenty-five years ago, a slot for each tenant, the cart's wood having accrued a gorgeous patina. He enjoyed casing the mail and became proficient at it. He rolled the cart onto the service car and left each day's delivery at a preordained spot, or handed it to a maid or houseman. He looked in on the animals of tenants, no problem, and walked a dog or two with pleasure. He thought the dogs of the rich lived particularly lonely lives.

He enjoyed the buffing machine when he worked midnights. Connie had guided such instruments across many a lobby floor. To do it right took patience. You could not force the machine to do your bidding, it would buck you like a wild horse, going on to crack the handcrafted molding at the base of the lobby wall, and to your super you would have to deny any knowledge of the divot created by a machine that in your demanding willfulness got away from you.

A good buff job required a pace and momentum all its own, the work fostering a meditative state, helping Connie to slow his mind down. He knew how to strip a floor to its essence, then raise it back up to perfection.

He offered to teach buffing workshops to his Local 32B union brothers, making official announcements in the locker room at its most crowded changeover hour. He let the guys know his availability for buffing tutorials should they be so inclined, and oh how his coworkers laughed. Connie laughed too. His sense of humor was a lifesaver.

He kept the machine's pads in good shape, letting them air out on hooks down in the slop-sink room. Doing a floor right brought Connie peace in the middle of the night and carried him through some rough psychic spots. The toxins would escape him as he worked, the lobby reeking of a low-rent gin mill for a period of time. He'd open the front doors wide and let the breeze sail in off the street. To work the buffer on a midnight shift, to do a good job in peace. He knew it wasn't some special skill to write home about, but like anybody else he enjoyed doing a thing well.

Whenever he started at a new house (he'd worked in half a dozen buildings the last ten years), he'd do the lobby floor to make a good first impression. He'd get those backless benches, wing-backed chairs, and side tables out of the way, furniture collectively purchased by the house's board after great stylistic wrangling and contention, and he'd strip the floor of all previous half-baked attempts, to that point when he could relish the floor's vulnerability, its nakedness exposed, its flat matte look devoid of shine. He'd stop and look out over the lobby, the unvarnished marble now exhibiting a profound frailty in Connie's eyes. He'd smoke a cigarette beneath the canopy, then start the rebuilding process, slowly throughout the night, one layer at a time, coat after coat, letting the toxins escape his pores.

After the bundles of *New York Times* and *Wall Street Journal* got dumped onto the sidewalk with a *thwap-thwap* from the back of a news truck, and the sky's last star went out, whatever super he worked for would appear from the back hall to question how his new man held up overnight, and upon seeing the floor could not hide his astonishment. And Connie with his tour de force buff job would be in like Flynn for a time, getting looked upon as the house's second coming, as one by one the tenants inquired as to the artisan's identity. They sought out Connie to offer deep appreciation, having had no idea how beautiful their lobby truly was before his talents revealed it to them.

"Thank you so much, Connie, you're a godsend."

"Pleasure," he'd say, which wasn't untrue.

Connie would ride that introductory buff job for as long as he could, while the rest of the staff walked around with stiff shorts, stiff with envy and paranoia, the unspoken threat of termination looming over them now, their building-maintenance fraud having come to light.

Imagine, all this time, the tenants mused, having to accept such lackluster results prior to Connie's arrival. What other mediocre efforts lurk and linger? Tenants would start to examine their residence with sharper eyes, coming and going, walking their manicured poodles and schnauzers, trying to make peace with all the power and wealth implied by their house's limestone edifice.

Connie's buff job confused them. *Is that the actual color of our canopy—or is it filthy? Perhaps we should petition Connie to investigate and have him perform one of his deep-scale transformations.*

And the staff's long-timers would think, *Who the hell does that son of a bitch think he is, to come in here and pull a buff job like that? Son of a no-good so-and-so.*

Then, sure enough, and sooner than later, Connie's shadow would start to stretch itself across the job, revealing the gaps in his character, allowing his coworkers to exhale. *Thank God,* they privately reflected, *he's human after all.*

He would start to show up late, or not at all, unable to perform his duties, citing an adverse reaction to medication. Most supers were decent. They wanted to believe Connie. He had kind eyes, which the shock of black hair exploding from his head helped frame like two mismatched stones of crazy lace agate set into his face. They'd have a little talk, then quietly send him home. They saw a good man beneath the bullshit and wanted to save his job. But what can you do with a guy who not only doesn't show up but doesn't call, or shows up half in the bag smelling like the kind of alcoholism no amount of Listerine will camouflage, or, maybe most perplexing, shows up sober and clean-shaven, dressed in a freshly pressed uniform and ready to work, only to discover it's his scheduled day off.

Eventually Connie would test the waters verbally with tenants and their guests, working himself into a proletarian huff. He would think people were starting to look at him funny, and would find himself embarrassed by his uniform, the embroidered bands of gold or silver on the cuffs of his jacket, and the piping down his pants. *I'm not a jockey outside some restaurant!* he would self-declare. He would begin to challenge the job's boundaries. Most tenants went out of their way to be respectful, yet it was true some could not help look down their nose, and Connie bit and snapped at those tenants. He would start cracking wise, a statement here or there concerning Tricky Dick, or the SLA, or some such, statements carrying currents of dark innuendo. And who needs that? From staff? Coming and going from your own home, having to run the meager gauntlet of an opinionated, inappropriately acerbic doorman? At one house he wasn't long for, Connie mistook a mother-in-law for a nanny, and as the lady waited to be picked up with her grandchild, Connie took the opportunity to present one of his working-class soliloquies. "See this, all this here?" he said, indicating the expansive lobby with a sweep of his arm. "Rubble, nothing but rubble, six to eight years, mark my words," he said, chuckling at his own pomposity, just as the mother-in-law, behind a tight smile, started to mentally orchestrate the steps required for Connie's departure.

This is how it went: he received numerous verbal warnings, followed by a handful of written warnings, before management and union reps got called in. They would have a sit-down in the super's office and Connie would get fired over some last-straw incident, with the caveat that another position would be secured, though any seniority was lost, which was fine with Connie, as he didn't believe in the future. It was uncanny in what similar ways these terminations played out. He got hired in another house managed by Douglas Elliman–Gibbons & Ives, or Brown Harris, and upon his arrival he'd rip the lobby floor a new ass, before frustrations would once again start to build, up to that point where he could no longer hold the spring down, and he'd work his way toward another dismissal.

The job, ultimately—and Connie knew this—required too little of him. In the case of his current employment, his tenure would last just under two years, similar in duration to his other positions. Within a short week he'd get fired for actions even his friends on the board could not excuse, and Connie's exit would spoil Walter's peace of mind for a month.

* * *

They played a variety of board games, a variety of card games, but they always came back to cribbage. Gin rummy and five-card stud and crazy eights. They tried games that called for the exchange of fake currency and found those games ridiculous.

"This money . . . it's . . . counterfeit," Connie said, giving the words ironic depth and discovery. John laughed and took a greedy hit off a bong he had bootlegged out of his room.

They played pinochle and backgammon and an Asian game called Go, territorial in nature, laying down stones on a grid board smooth to the touch. They played Yahtzee and blackjack, chess and checkers, but cribbage was their mainstay.

John rang whichever car Connie worked, the front or back. Connie swung the door open and the kid stood there, a look of hope in his eyes and a mouth full of braces.

"Game of crib, Con, a little later maybe?" John said.

He lived on the fifteenth floor, but they hung out in the back stairwell of the house's ninth floor, a spot they dubbed The Office. A two-tone, high-gloss battleship-gray painted the walls, a lemony disinfectant scented the air. A Swiss family who owned the ninth floor came into town one week a year in the fall, maybe a week in the summer—otherwise nine was dead.

"Let's see what's what," Connie said. "I got to clear a couple dockets, but my guess, we could squeeze a few games in," and this speech bogus: there was always time for some cribbage.

The building had twenty-seven units on seventeen floors, and with a staff of sixteen, even though nobody came right out and said it, this house was a piece of cake.

Time could be found for a couple rounds of cribbage, never mind a nap in your favorite hideaway spot that hurt who, exactly?

The kid was lonely in that thirteen-year-old way, moving through a transitional period, hoping to shed a piece of his childhood, trying to step into something along the lines of what might be considered a young manhood, maybe?

He missed his sister. They used to ditch their Secret Service detail together—two little potheads out among the sordid throngs of Times Square. Who else could fathom their history but each for the other? The circumstances of their lives forged them together by blood, their connection shorthand and symbiotic.

She lived at boarding school in Massachusetts these days, and his mother had started to spend more weekends in Washington. Frankly, the mother didn't know what to do with him and this attitude of his lately, which left John and the governess to pad around the apartment's nineteen rooms.

They played on a board given to him for his eighth birthday, an heirloom of sorts, his father's surreal initials branded into the back of its antique wood. The original pegs had gone missing, so they used matchsticks that worked just fine. They talked and laughed and appreciated each other's company. They shot the breeze about sports. They smoked Connie's Camels and the kid's stash of reefer. They unfolded two stools, a foldout table, and created a foldout world.

Connie didn't go strange. Most people in John's life, they met him and their faces did something. By the age of five he spotted it, the people who jumped out of their bodies and went strange on him. They had a hatful of ideas, a thousand and one ideas about him. *They can't see me*, John thought. Okay, not everyone gets to meet Muhammad Ali, he understood that. Still. *I'm a kid*, he thought. *My father's dead, a lot of people are dead, what do you* want? Even the coolest of customers tried to see behind his eyes, and John thought, *You can't see behind my eyes.*

Give me a goddamn break, he whispered to the world. He had fallen away from any genuine connection to his peers. He'd get high in the park with a crowd out behind the museum, but he didn't consider them friends, really. He didn't know what was going on just lately, and since when for a thirteen-year-old is that a crime?

Not last summer but the summer before, Connie swung the elevator open onto the lobby and John stood there, skin roasted brown, hair streaked by the Mediterranean sun, this before his mother's scene in Greece had come to an end. They looked at each other a moment.

"Coming in or what?" Connie said.

John stepped into the car, Connie swung the gate shut and dipped the lever. "Where you going?"

"Fifteen," John said.

Connie took him up, and after some quiet said, "Can you keep a secret?"

"Yeah," John said.

"Hungover like a son of a bitch."

John laughed.

"Do me a favor," Connie said, "you get in the house, think you could scramble me up a couple aspirin?"

"Sure," John said, and found himself making a direct line to the medicine cabinet.

"What do I owe you?" Connie said.

"On the house," John said.

"You're the best," Connie said, not strange at all, and Connie liked the kid because he thought to bring a glass of water with the aspirin.

Connie had the modest talent of bringing the car flush to a floor and swinging the gate open all in one fluid motion and with a certain comical panache. "Bang, you see that? No herky-jerky," he would say. "Don't believe in herky-jerky, against my religion."

He let John run the elevator. "Take over. Watch your hand at the gate."

A simple trust established itself, not a big deal, an in-house friendship limited to the parameters of the building.

"Game of crib, Con, a little later maybe?"

"Can you handle the agony of defeat?"

"In your dreams!"

The kid, it's true, had uncles and cousins and friends of the family with stories to tell about the old man, but at the end of the day was he not fatherless?

The Secret Service called him Lark. John disliked it.

Up in the ninth floor's back stairwell, just after lunch, Connie started to fade.

"You okay, Con?"

"Let's break this party up," Connie said. "See if I can hit the bags for forty winks." He took naps on bags of mixing cement down in the basement.

Funny thing: Connie didn't know who John was until after they had played cards and John had gotten him high a few times. Something in Connie refused to make the recognition. Not until John stepped into the elevator with his mother one day did the identification fully register. The mother, with her height and sunglasses, and the singular glamor of her encroaching middle-age beauty, was hard-pressed to pull off a stab at anonymity.

So the friendship of Connie and John established itself before Fame could work its voodoo—otherwise Connie might have gone strange himself. The starry-eyed often make the famous feel as if they're getting jumped: if anyone's ever rifled through your pockets without permission, it might offer a clue as to the burdens of celebrity. Many Americans wanted to use him to bolster some romantic national myth of their own, but even as a very young person John sensed its falseness and shunned the role.

In his dreams Connie endured old sorrows and loss, powered not by fleshed-out dramatic scenarios but the tableau stillness of sepia portraits his dream-eye slowly dollied past, taking in the faces of family and friends long dead, the faces of strangers mixed in as well. His dead mother, Mary. His dead father, Samuel. His youngest brother, Edward, dead at two and a half—all of them gone now, never to be seen again, not on earth, not in heaven, hell, or purgatory. *Only in my dreams*, Connie dreamed, *can I see you.*

He sat as a nine-year-old cross-legged in the dream, handcuffed to the radiator in the bedroom of the Harlem apartment where he and his mother, his brothers Patrick and Danny, and his half sister Ruth had lived for six months, a time and place which included the passing of their father and Edward. And on the tragedy's heels came their mother's new husband, Pete Cullen: the name after all these years still charged with the darkest of freight in Connie's psyche.

Connie had in reality been handcuffed as a kid, but never to that apartment's radiator. He started to cry with intense dream-grief. His body, curled on the bags of mixing cement down in the basement, shivered tightly. His mouth flooded with saliva. Footsteps approached. Images from the dream would return as he smoked on the sidewalk during intermission of a play he would second-act in a few nights, a show at the Morosco Theatre starring Jason Robards and Colleen Dewhurst.

He slept for twenty minutes and, despite the dream's turbulence, woke refreshed. The cement bags, placed deliberately between the tenants' storage cages, catered well to the contours of his body, offering just the right give. He yawned and stretched. The footsteps came to a stop. Francis Ramey looked down at him.

"May I help you?" Connie said, wondering if the smell of unmixed cement influenced his dreamscape.

"They pay you to sleep?" Ramey said.

"What do you want?"

"Toilet paper."

Prior to meeting Ramey and his partner Henry Slovell, Connie assigned the qualities of stoic dignity and disciplined commitment to the Secret Service, but this changed with the reality of his dealings with them, especially Ramey. Slovell rarely exited their government-issued Impala, sitting beneath a weeping willow on the park side of Fifth. Complementing their presence were two containers of coffee from the Greeks wedged between the dash and windshield and a never-ending ball game on the radio.

Connie didn't care for Ramey, not only because he thought they dropped the ball when it came to protecting

John. Ramey reminded Connie of a kid who sat behind him in homeroom for the month he attended ninth grade at Cardinal Hayes High School, a granite-winged structure up on the Bronx's Grand Concourse. This kid had tapped Connie's desk with his foot, and for Connie, Ramey and the kid descended from the same bloodline of arrogance.

"Nerve, making comments like you do."

"Is that right?"

Connie got to his feet. He tucked in his shirt, moving past a series of storage cages containing lonely armchairs and loose-wired fixtures. He stopped. "Don't cast aspersions on the job I do."

Ramey walked by him, and Connie followed.

"Now that I think about it," Connie said, staring at Ramey's back, "who are you to judge the caliber of my work?"

Connie caught himself reaching for a higher lexicon. *Aspersions. Caliber.* Ramey and the kid who foot-tapped his desk at Hayes both possessed a threatening look in their eyes, and Connie figured both of them had grown up with fathers who drove a sense of unwarranted superiority into them. He wanted to stove Ramey's head in with a pipe and see what his face looked like then.

"Walk around like you own the joint," Connie said.

"I do, far as you're concerned."

"Oh, is that right?"

"That is right."

Ramey looked at him as Connie took the lead again, walking by the washer machines nobody much used, when Connie stopped and unlocked the supply closet. He reached up to a shelf for a roll of toilet paper, turned, and tossed it to Ramey.

Ramey walked down the hall, entered the bathroom, clicked the lock behind him, and through the door Connie barely caught it but he did hear it when Ramey said, "Little drunk."

"Say what?" Connie called.

"Like it takes the Secret Service to figure that one out."

Connie jiggled the loose change in his pocket in search of some retort, but came up empty.

Connie on the housephone called upstairs, where Walter tried to fix a tenant's broken music box—a smallish model of a French Alps chalet, replete with snowcapped roof. Walter turned the piece over in his hands with innocent curiosity, a little like King Kong.

The tenant offered Walter leftover sandwiches from her bridge game. He declined, wondering if the lady did not understand he was of Italian heritage. Some mayo salad thing, little white bread squares, no crust—*you putting me on or what?*

"Thinking about taking off," Connie said on the phone. "Need me to do anything before I hit it?"

"Go ahead," Walter said. The fact that Connie sought him out before departing wasn't lost on Walter—most of these guys scurried away at shift's end. *He sees my humanity*, Walter thought with fondness, *I can talk to him.*

Connie popped out through the service entrance. He went to his spot on Lex and picked up a pint, came back west, and meandered his way south through the park, stopping for a moment to admire a family of ducks motoring by on the reservoir.

Thank God for hip pockets. Just knowing he had a

taste on hand, the bottle safely deployed on him, its sensuous curve snuggled up good and tight against his own body, was oftentimes in and of itself enough to quiet the storm, the otherwise nonstop psychic brouhaha that ran him ragged. Connie's goal: to maintain a steady hum that would prevent him from slipping off the planet.

Of course he frequently overshot or, just as troubling, undershot this course of maintenance. He had over the years encountered people here and there who did not indulge and marveled at them. He'd stand back and watch them refrain and scratch his head, unable to conceive it, unable finally to trust such individuals. Safe to say, he was not a take-it-or-leave-it drinker—it was intricately woven into the fabric of his days, he lived in bars—and though he had a rule never to feed them money (except on the rare occasion to impress the odd, stray drunk woman toward the four a.m. hour), he shamefully relished the sounds of the jukebox, all the pity songs, the repertoire of lost love, the chronicles of yearning: music, every sloppy lick of it, geared to pump your chest with the surging, pathetic flood of remorse.

As Connie headed toward the park's bandshell he stopped to observe a brown-muscled Doberman stalk a squirrel, the Dobie's nose down close to the hexagonal stones of the promenade. It crept up in predatory style on the distracted squirrel, playing all alone at the base of a tree. The dog snatched it by its back, squeezed it in its jaws, shook it, let it drop. It looked down at the lifeless squirrel, glanced around embarrassed, before trotting back toward its owner, a woman whose face lay half-obscured beneath a floppy hat. She carried an L.L.Bean tote, wore a pair of Wallabees and a peacoat purchased, to judge from its cut, not at Alexander's or Klein's, but Saks or Bergdorf, Connie surmised. Over-dressed for mid-May, her lips parted slightly with the hint of satisfaction. Connie sensed she lived vicariously through the animal, the glint of murderous delight alive in the woman's eyes.

Connie was a fan of *Mutual of Omaha's Wild Kingdom*, the TV show hosted by Marlin Perkins, and had CliffsNotes comprehension of Darwinian theory, but something about this squirrel's gratuitous death disturbed him, how the dog's owner maybe encouraged it.

He thought he had heard the sound of the squirrel's bones crack in the dog's mouth but wasn't sure if his mind made it up. He produced his pint and washed these thoughts down.

"Hey, Mr. Doorman," some kids called, "over here."

Connie turned toward the bandshell.

"Come on over," they called.

Moving through clouds of patchouli and marijuana, Connie approached the hippie kids who acid-tripped there. They hung out in small clusters, a United Nations of teenagers, black and white, Jewish and Puerto Rican. They passed around joints and sweaty quarts of Olde English 800. Couples cradled each other with the tenderness of youth and made out off to the side. They drank and got high and listened to *Let It Bleed*.

Connie went to the four-pack of kids who called to him. They sat downstage right, letting their legs dangle and bounce.

"Nice uniform," a girl with frizzy hair said.

"I smell reefer," Connie said, and they laughed.

"Want to get high?" a ponytailed kid said.

"Yes please," he said, and they laughed some more.

From a small manila envelope the kid shook some pot onto the bandshell's stone stage and started to separate out seeds and twigs. He got the pot good and clean before he crumpled it up into a smokable grain. With a soft matchbook cover he scooped it up and sprinkled it into a single folded sheet of Bambú. They watched the joint get rolled in silence, bearing witness to a sacred ritual. He sealed it with a lick, stuck the thing in his mouth, then held the joint up to air-dry a moment, before he extended it to Connie with just a subtle show of ceremony.

"Thank you, sir," Connie said. "I like your style."

Connie put it in his mouth, flipped open his Zippo, and brought its wild flame toward the joint with respectful caution, as he did not want to light it haphazardly and thereby waste any of the precious herb. He gave it a thorough toke and held the smoke in with theatrical flair, his eyes blinking, doing this and that, and the kids got a kick out of the guy, probably even over thirty, maybe, in his doorman's uniform, getting high with them, and Connie could tell they were good kids. They were different than the kids in the projects in that they had been afforded the chance to develop a greater gentleness of spirit, which he found attractive. They came from homes with books and record collections and art on the walls, you could just tell. Their parents were doctors or lawyers, teachers or artists, and perhaps a few of the kids in the crowd were from the projects or tenements, kids naturally drawn to a more kind and literate scene. This crowd had genuine Swiss Army knives in belted leather sheaths, and wore Italian hiking boots that cost sixty-five dollars at Paragon, and the pot's quality was stellar.

He passed the joint and held the smoke in his lungs. Without exhaling he said, "Good stuff," and the kids laughed. He choked and sputtered from deep inside his chest. Finally, he let it go, bent over, and caught his breath. He stood up straight, produced his pint, and took a hit.

"Who wants a taste, anybody?" Connie said, and they looked at him. "Wow," he said, "discriminating palates." Connie spotted a kid spinning a Frisbee on his finger upstage. "Yo, yo, with the Frisbee and the 'fro!" he called, then broke from the four-pack of kids and started to sprint between the wrought-iron chairs sitting vacant and scattershot before the bandshell.

The Afroed kid watched Connie break into his long pattern, grinned big, and with a short one-two-three-step release let the Frisbee rip. It flew up and off the stage as Connie zigged and zagged through the wrought-iron chairs. The Frisbee soared and they all watched him work to track it down, calling, "Go, Mr. Doorman, go!"

A desperation fueled Connie, and something in him, now that he had committed, wanted to make the grab. He felt emotions he had not experienced in years, a single-minded intensity that sport produced, wherein all internal clutter falls away. His head and chest pounded as the rhythm of his stride began to synch up with the Frisbee, they were one and the same, and the bandshell kids picked up on it, calling to Connie with ever greater excitement.

"You got it, Doorman, you got it!"

He had to negotiate a few stand-alone garbage cans and a couple of human beings—a homeless man and a bald-headed toddler on the loose—when a wind came, a gust from nowhere, and the Frisbee hovered midair. The kids made noise to guide and direct.

"Ho, Doorman, wait up! Ho!"

The Frisbee tried to make up its mind, before it slowly, with coy prerogative, reversed gears and started back toward the bandshell.

"Back, Doorman, back, back!"

Connie retraced his path and the Frisbee picked up speed, boomeranging its way toward the bandshell with a fickle change of heart, and with the turnabout Connie caught a second wind, hissing under his breath, "You motherless son of a." He spoke to the Frisbee, gave the thing its own volition and consciousness, he conjured the Frisbee into a supercilious bitch of a human being. "Pull that shit on me," he said. He again negotiated the wrought-iron chairs but the effort less than half as hard now, needing only an inverse take on a course his body had intuitively retained, as the Frisbee descended, descended.

"Watch it, Doorman, watch it!" the kids cried.

The Doberman that had taken the squirrel's life galloped at him from a disturbingly obtuse angle. And Connie thought, *If it bites me, it bites me, I'm not scared of dogs, never have been*, and the Dobie vanished like cowards always do.

Down the Frisbee came, and with it Connie downshifted—it was going to happen now, the wind had dissipated—and the kids smiled for Connie, the grab was imminent, but for no discernible reason he overshot the thing and the kids flashed sad Connie had blown it at the last moment . . . when he took them unawares with a behind-the-back snatch which blew their minds, just as he spun and quick-flipped it back to the Afroed kid upstage, having possessed the Frisbee for no amount of time worth counting, and the upstage kid caught it where he stood.

They slapped each other five, hugged, and shook their bodies. A tall kid with a soul patch placed a hand on Connie's shoulder and said, "That was so cool." He offered a quart of Olde English and Connie took a victorious guzzle.

"Later, kids."

"Come back soon, Mr. Doorman," they called.

Connie waved goodbye, and he never did return to them.

South he roamed on pedestrian paths, gently swaying this way and that. He stopped to watch a shaft of light infiltrate a canopy of green, the trees leaning, the branches reaching with desire for one another above him. How the light landed on a boulder just off the path. Like a painting at the Met Connie took in on a recent rainy lunch break. But this, the actual sun and trees of the world, and the sight of it spoke to the unschooled artist in him. He considered the stains on the boulder, the mildew, tried to regard the shapes not as some Rorschach for his longings, but something which had nothing to do with him personally, like a painting hanging in the Met.

He left the park at Columbus Circle. The marquee of the Coliseum read *Boat Show*, and a few salesmen in loosened, fat-knotted ties and one minidressed woman stood smoking together outside. From their countenance Connie decided they hadn't written much business at all.

One of Connie's brothers, Patrick, a teamster, worked the Coliseum. Connie rarely spoke to his siblings; even throughout the holidays the last number of years it stayed quiet between them. They suffered such decimation when they were children that the brothers and half sister Ruth seemed to prefer no contact, as spending time together only served to rehash a past better left to wither on the vine. The suicide of their father, the negligent homicide of baby brother Edward, followed by the violence of Pete Cullen, its horror doubled by their mother's inability to protect—all this could not help but flood its way back when they saw one another. When they did get together, the result of some spouse's insistence, it produced in Connie a hangover of shame which lingered for a week that no amount of booze dissolved. Still, whenever he walked by the Coliseum he naturally thought of Patrick, who now lived, Connie believed, in Bronxville with a Spanish wife and kids. He thought of Danny and Ruth as well, and the memories of his brother Edward, and what a kick he used to get as a kid himself holding Edward in his arms.

He loved to walk the streets of Manhattan, and Brooklyn too (he loved the generous, open skies of Brooklyn, it was always what he first noticed coming up out of the trains). He would hate to consider a day when he could not step out and just start walking, a simple pleasure which had yet to fizzle or fade.

He headed down Ninth Avenue, passing Port Authority and the fruit stands, when it hit him: he no longer had a place to call home. He managed to put this out of his mind. It happened this morning, did it not?

A sadness accosted him, as post office drivers in their elevated cabs careened their trucks rudely across his path into the loading dock. His sense of destination abruptly dissolved. *Where am I going?* he thought.

He produced his house key, recalling the door's new cylinder, and the memory collapsed over him. He removed the key from its ring and surreptitiously brought it to his nose—the smell rancid, metallic. He crossed the avenue and, as he did, let the key fall from his hand, and he thought, *Maybe the sun will soften the pavement and downtown traffic'll punish the key into the tar. And whenever I'm on Ninth I'll see the key embedded in the street and only I will know what door it used to open. I'll remember how I let it slip from my hand, May of '74, and how the key represented my failed shot at love and family.*

His mind revved up for its blunt assault: Never should have tried it. Should have left well enough alone and never brought other people into the mix. Should have stayed a bachelor. A room in a rooming house. Falafels, pizza slices, Chinese takeout and double features in dark movie houses to muscle your way through long holiday weekends alone.

He cut through what was known in the neighborhood as Bums Park, the centerpiece of the space a free city health clinic, a squat three-story structure surrounded by strange homeless nomads with wild hair who slept on benches. Children were notoriously frightened to enter its confines, the dangers of which had taken on mythological proportions.

One bearded man in an army jacket talked quietly to himself on a bench across the way: Tommy Dunn. Connie had known him forever. Tommy got kicked out of the projects—not an easy thing to do. *How do you lose a project apartment, Tommy? If I had a nickel for every time Tommy made somebody laugh*, Connie thought.

Don't get Tommy started on you in front of a crowd, watch out! And it was a good humor. Deeply offensive, yes, deeply racist, sure it was, but somehow devoid of malice or vitriol. *There is love underneath it, isn't there, Tom?* Tommy'd stroll up to half a dozen guys sitting around a concrete checker table and just start riffing. What a natural, what an athlete. And now? Relegated to a bench in Bums Park, clutching a pint of MD 20/20, a knotty beard of chaos defacing him.

God Almighty, Tom, what did they do to you?

They used to shoot the breeze when they encountered each other, spent a good twenty minutes catching up, but now Connie prayed to go unnoticed, as Tommy represented a frightening projection of his own potential future.

Connie cut past the sandbox and basketball court, the monkey bars and swings, the horseshoe pits and handball courts of Chelsea Park, before he leaned against the fence on 27th Street and peered into the thickening fog of the softball field. He wondered how they could still see the puck, but as the sun had gradually set over the Hudson, the kids developed night vision.

He spotted Arthur. The informal roller hockey scrimmage had started to dissolve. Kids on opposing teams stopped skating to talk to one another. The goalies stood bored between two garbage cans, hoping for the chance to make one more Eddie Giacomin–style save before calling it a day.

Connie listened to Arthur teach a younger player how to spear somebody, his words drifting across the field. Arthur told the kid he should only spear a player who messed with him, that the kid shouldn't do it just for fun.

Use your spearing skills judiciously was Arthur's point.

"Say I messed with you all game, so you go digging for the puck and I'm coming up behind you." Arthur produced a roll of electrical tape from inside his glove and let it drop to the ground. "Ready?" he said, and fired a snap-shot against the fence near Connie. The kid dug hard and fearless for it with Arthur bearing down. "Stick in position," Arthur said, and the kid lowered his grip on the butt and centered it behind him in a manner which would prevent a player from crushing him into the boards. "Good," Arthur said, and smacked the kid's stick out of the way and crunched him anyway.

"Hey," the kid said, laughing.

Arthur banged him into the fence with a dry humor, not for real, not too aggressive. The kid was smaller and younger than Arthur. Arthur kept playing dumb, saying, "What?"

"Hey!" the kid said, laughing again, and Arthur continued to crunch the kid, but when he looked up and saw his father, he stopped and skated away.

"Arthur," Connie said.

"Hey, Mr. Sky," the kid said.

"How you doing, son?" Connie said to the kid. "Arthur, come here a minute."

"What?" Arthur said.

"Meet me over the hole."

Somebody had cut a hole in the fence. Arthur skated reluctantly toward it as Connie walked that way, the fence dividing them.

"Still playing," Arthur said.

"I know," Connie said, "want to talk to you a minute." He slid through the gap and stood with Arthur, who skated in small, choppy circles. "Come here, can't see you."

"Yeah, 'cause it's dark."

"Want to get some dinner?"

"Can't."

"Come on, couple slices."

"Mommy's cooking," Arthur said. "Told her I'd be there."

"All right, all right," Connie said. "Well then, let's just talk."

"About what?" Arthur started to skate in faster circles, smacking the blade of his stick down onto the ground harder.

Connie said, "Stop with the stick, going to crack it," and Arthur obeyed for the moment, almost grateful for the instruction. "Listen. Your mother and me."

"I know, I know."

"What do you know?"

"Separating, she told me."

"For now," Connie said. "Temporary."

"Until when?"

"Until we see what's what is when," Connie said.

"Yeah, right."

"Yeah, right, what?"

Arthur sniffed the air. "Nothing."

"Say it," Connie said, "it's all right."

Arthur stayed quiet.

"What is it?"

Arthur took a glove off and wiped his face, snorting back a sudden flash-flood mélange of tears and snot and saliva. "Yeah, right, what, okay—and like I wish you were dead already," Arthur said, "that's what's fucking what," and he skated away.

"Arthur," Connie said.

Arthur kept skating. "Die already, get it the fuck over with. I hate you. Find a bench, leave us alone already, if that's how you're going to be already."

"Arthur!" Connie called out. "Artie!"

"No!" Arthur yelled across the park. "Banging on the door like that! Don't love us! And I'm not going to your funeral either, tell you that shit right now!"

The sound of Arthur's stick slapping the ground grew more distant until Connie lost him, sight and sound, to the fog. He stood there for a moment, half hoping Arthur would return to do who knows what—apologize, say worse things, or skate into Connie's arms and cry his eyes out.

Thick white clouds had descended, filling the space, white zeppelins straight from the Hudson, landing in Chelsea Park.

Connie stood still. There had been words between himself and Arthur throughout the last number of months, but none like what he just heard. The kid had found a strong voice. *I hate you,* Arthur had said. Wished Connie was dead.

Connie listened to some kids at a distance skating home for dinner. The fog grew thicker. He stood there, short of breath, strangely exhilarated. A fog-cloaked stillness filled the park, muting the world. So little open space in the neighborhood, on the island of Manhattan altogether, the fog seemed thankful to have found a spot to do its thing. How nice would that be? Scooped up and carried out on a bed of fog, sliding beneath the belly of the Verrazano, right on out to sea.

Connie listened to the sound of his own breathing,

stunned by Arthur's tumult. And with it also a strange pride for his son. He sensed Arthur was onto something, glad the kid had found words for it, managed to fire it out of him.

He could teach me a thing or two . . . I never got angry, did I? I forgot to get angry.

What was my father's name again? A wiry man they called Jumbo. But his name—his name was Samuel. Sammy.

Samuel Sky, the printer. That's what he did, what Connie's mimeographed birth certificate said, the one Connie discovered in a brown file of corrugated cardboard hidden deep in his mother's closet, searching through it as his mother smoked her Salems out on the stoop in her one iconic housecoat of impoverishment. Trying to glean some information about his own father from the shadowed document. *My father*, Connie thought, *the printer. Turned the oven on, late afternoon, January 19, 1951. This side of dusk, first star in the sky. Turned the oven on and took baby brother Edward with him.*

Connie adjusted his cap, and for a moment considered himself a captain on the bow of a ship in the middle of a fog-shrouded ocean. He stepped deeper into the thickening fog, in search of its epicenter. The ground of the softball field rocking slightly beneath him, the cigarette in his hand not visible, save the faint glow of its tip, the glow of a distant lighthouse between two fingers.

Kid had a lot of nerve, he thought. *Little punk. Lucky you got a father. If I took myself out, then maybe. Let me pull a suicide. Then the kid might have something to smack the blade of his stick down on the ground about. Talk to me like that on the street. Pull that shit on me.*

He moved deeper into the field, fog-blinded. Now

came the soft *toot-toot* of a car horn on Tenth Avenue, not a sound of impatience, but a gentle, caring goodbye, to and from a loved one, Connie decided.

Here I stand, blind to the world. And if I went missing for good, who would mourn me? He surrendered to his pity, took a hit off his pint, let the fog envelope him. He stood captured by it, white and blinding, blinding wet and white.

One day over a round of cribbage John out of the blue said, "What did your father do? You know, for a job."

"My father," Connie said. "When he did work, he was a printer."

"In what, a printing plant?"

"Down the docks of Chelsea." And as he nonchalantly considered the cards in his hand, Connie said, "What'd your father do?"

John grinned. "My father? Public service. Yeah. Like a family business." He grabbed Connie's Zippo off the table, opened and banged its small rough wheel against his leg in one fluid quick-draw motion, producing a flame toward which he brought a fresh joint.

Steven called Alfonso "Fonso." Nobody's name needed three syllables when you were nine years old, come on. Steven and Alfonso were best friends, simple as that. Alfonso, part Panamanian, had a football-shaped head, small teeth, and large gums. These physical oddities in no way put a halt to Alfonso's vanity. The kid was full of himself and stayed on perpetual alert for a chance at physical self-reflection, often stopping to take advantage of a parked car's side-view mirror, even a puddle in the gutter.

Steven sat on a bench by the skelsies board Alfonso had meticulously designed with large, round pieces of chalk in the yard of 466. Alfonso ran the board and Steven waited.

Alfonso possessed substantial skelly skills, and he created superbad caps, mixing and matching his waxes, producing psychedelic results. Both boys stayed on the lookout for new cap possibilities. Lately they had discovered a series of chairs at PS 33, not in the classrooms but in the offices where the secretary lady and nurse lady sat, chairs with particular knobs on their leg bottoms: made of silver, they carried a good, balanced weight, and seemed born to glide. The challenge was to not get busted. Messing with school property—they didn't like that. Steven and Alfonso took turns keeping chickie.

Alfonso was serious and fastidious and took all kinds of extra time setting up his shots, not a trace of chalk on the kid's clothes. Whereas Steven's T-shirts always had a stain, he could not draw for beans, and the wax in his cap collection was unbalanced and generally unattractive.

"Daddy!" Steven jumped off the bench and ran like a shot toward Connie.

Connie embraced and kissed him. "How you doing, son?" A lady up in Harlem who wore a red bandanna and lived across the street had called Connie *son*. She took his face in her dry, black hands, and Connie always wondered if she knew about Pete Cullen, if that was the reason she showed Connie love, or was it simply who she was?

They went and sat on the bench and watched Alfonso run the board, his cap slowly sliding to rest smack dab in the middle of each box.

"Nice," Steven said.

"Good shooting there, Mr. Alfonso," Connie said.

Alfonso roamed the board's periphery, paving the way for each shot's trajectory, reaching down to pluck away some invisible piece of debris like a golfer on a green.

Steven's legs swung with impatience, and he gave his father a look and made the smallest *cluck* sound with his tongue, to which Alfonso stopped and said: "What?!"

"Take so long! Just shoot, know you're going to make it."

Connie slept with Alfonso's mother Melba years ago, during a long night of partying. She had large breasts and wore eyeglasses. Melba got on top of Connie and gyrated, and as she did she sucked on one of her own knuckles, which Connie found to be an open and generous display of her sexuality. Baby Alfonso asleep in a crib across the room, back when Melba's mom lived with them. Melba gave him a kiss at the door, and whispered, *No more, it's wrong, I like Maureen.*

"Stevie, listen: Mommy home?"

"Uh-huh. Going up?"

"Me and Mommy, we're having a few problems."

"I know."

"You do?"

Steven exploded off the bench, saying, "On the line, on the line, on the line," just as Alfonso himself jumped back, saying, "Na, na, na, na," pointing to his cap, saying, "It's in, it's in, it's in, it's in, from here you can, come on," to which Steven said, "Trust you, trust you, trust you, trust you," before plopping back down onto the bench.

Connie waited a moment and said, "How do you know?"

"Changed the lock is why," Steven whispered, his voice going hollow at the center. "'Cause your drinking and how you wet the bed, she said, and the fooling around and stuff like that, how she said on the phone to Aunt Carol and all them."

"Listen to me now: I love Mommy and Mommy loves me, and I love you and Artie, nothing's ever going to change that, bottom line, no matter what."

"I know," Steven said, barely audible.

"Period, end of story," Connie said, and waited for Steven to kick in with his part. It was a routine of theirs.

"Cut and dried, my friend," Steven said, but his heart wasn't in it.

"Day you were born, that deal went down hard," Connie said, hugging Steven to him. The deal being Connie would love his son forever and always, no questions asked, no doubt about it, the deal gone down, day you were born, cut and dried my friend, my son, my beautiful boy. "Stevie, would you shoot upstairs and let Mommy know I want to pick up a couple things?"

"Right now?"

"If you don't mind."

"Take my place?" Steven said, jutting his face toward the skelsies board.

"If he gives me a chance."

"I know, Fonso's good," he said, then jumped up and ran toward the entrance of 466. "My father takes my place, Fonso!"

Connie lit a smoke and watched Alfonso. The kid had a humorous way about him. So neat. "When's my turn?"

"If I mess up," Alfonso said, making his way around the board like a pool hall hustler. He had the touch, and after each successful flick-shot he snapped his fingers.

"You're good, Alfonso."

"I know," he said, and Connie laughed, and as Alfonso set up his next shot he said: "My father, he was a doorman too," saying it almost as a question.

"I think he was," Connie said tentatively. "He worked over at London Terrace. A good man, your father, Alfonso. Very talented, like you."

"Like how?"

"You name it, like how. Played softball. Some shortstop."

"For real?" Alfonso said, glancing now at Connie.

"He could draw too, like you. Always with his pencil."

Alfonso's father one day up and disappeared, and who better than Connie to know about a father gone missing.

Here came Steven, and behind him Maureen, splitting off to the middle of the yard, carrying a black Hefty bag to keep it from scraping the ground. She stopped and waited by the Saturn sculpture.

"She's there," Steven said, pointing. "My turn?"

"Yeah," Alfonso said, "to warm that bench some more."

Maureen looked around in anticipation of an ambush. Or maybe she was just beat down by her weary marriage. Something about the language of her body seemed new to Connie, her stride, a defeat in her step. Yes, she looked drained, but also, beneath the exhaustion, signs of something which posed a subtle threat to Connie, and he couldn't pin it down.

She rested the Hefty bag on the ground and reached for the ring of Saturn with both hands, and Connie noticed her manicure as he approached. She stretched her legs and back as if in preparation for a long run.

"How you doing, Maureen?"

"Some of your things in the bag," she said. "Everything from the bathroom, a bunch of your clothes. Want to take a look, see if there's anything else you need for now?"

"What, I can't come up and go through my own things?"

"Prefer you didn't."

"Why's that?"

"You're not welcome in the house anymore." She shot a mindful look across the way at Steven, who pretended to watch Alfonso run the skelsies board.

The trees shimmered in the yard. Maureen glanced up at the identical brown roller-shaded windows, smacking of institutional ennui.

"You don't know what it does to the kids. Pounding on the door like that, middle of the night. I hope you don't know, 'cause if you knew and still did it? Stevie's happy-go-lucky, but when you're out there banging at four in the morning, loaded to the gills? And the other one, forget about," she said. "I'm worried about Arthur, Con, honestly."

"But you changed the locks."

"That's right."

"Why did you—"

"To keep you the hell out," Maureen said with a mock laugh.

Connie considered her, her tight jeans and sneakers and sweatshirt. Her hair. The manicure. He thought, *She's turned a corner.*

He always thought he had lucked into Maureen for a lover, a partner, a wife. From the start, the softest of spots responded to her in him, their sex a deeply spiritual communion unlike any Connie had ever known. He felt he could not have loved her more. They had once fucked the legs off a kitchen table, Connie watching one of the legs pogo-sticking its way out of the room in fear of further fucking as they hovered midair, a frozen moment on the tabletop like out of some cartoon, before collapsing down onto the floor in a heap together, still connected, laughing in shock and wonder, where they kept on fucking.

"I mean, who gives a shit, I'm still paying the rent," he said. "So what, I'm a little disjointed."

"Disjointed altogether, only you don't have a clue. And I'm fed up. For real now."

Connie reached for her hand, and Maureen pulled away.

"Hell are you doing?" she said. "Out of your mind."

"All right, look," he said, "are you saying we're done for good, or what?"

"Forget for good."

"Well then, or what?" he said, not knowing what he meant.

"Been done for good for years, Con. Years. Listen to me."

"And what about the kids?"

"Let's keep the kids out of it. Here's the deal: you say, *Are we done for good?* I say, *I don't know.* I changed the lock for a reason, not some whim, okay? I'm tired, Con. I can't take it anymore. You got a bad problem, and I cannot sit around and watch you. It's simple: tired of you wetting the bed. Tired of you sleeping around. I don't know another way to say it. Tired of our life together, it's a joke."

"All right," Connie said, "I hear you."

"Hear me? This conversation's older than the hills, pregnant with Arthur, you kidding me? Don't get me started. Point is, you say, *Are we done for good?* I say, *Who knows?* I'm not looking that far down the road. You go do what you have to do, show up for the kids, get the booze out of the picture. I don't want to tell you what to do, but if you're drinking . . . You just shouldn't drink, Con, honest to God. Forget it, if the drink's still in the picture. You show up as a father, and who knows, maybe we meet up again down the road, who's to say? You might not like me by that point. And I'm not laying it all on you, God knows I'm no angel. But for now I'm done. I can't anymore. You sober up, show up for the kids, and more than that I can't say."

Connie watched her a moment. He sensed she'd been talking to somebody, a friend, somebody. He knew he didn't have a leg to stand on, yet his mind continued to balk.

"You need help, hon," she said, and if she'd been on the phone you wouldn't know she was crying. "You need help, I need help. The kids . . ." she said, turning from Steven's eyes. "Find a place to stay?"

"Yeah," he lied.

"All right, so take the bag." She turned and headed back upstairs. "And stop walking around in that uniform." She said it over her shoulder, an afterthought, and Connie felt it betrayed a proprietary interest she maintained toward him.

He went over to the skelsies game, kissed and hugged

Steven. He gripped Alfonso lovingly by his football-shaped head, before he strolled through the yard toward Tenth Avenue.

Steven watched his father walk away, the Hefty bag tossed over his shoulder.

With invigorated purpose Connie moved toward Grant's Bar at the corner of 25th and Tenth. On his lips, the cooling vespers of hate: "Let them all go fuck themselves," his ironic tone that of a lighthearted ditty, and by *them* he meant his wife Maureen and his son Arthur, but not his son Steven. Also, as to who else might go fuck themselves, his dead parents, Mary and Samuel. And Pete Cullen, of course. This the main cast of characters on whose hooks his mind presently hung its anger, but the sentiment simultaneously held open an invitation to every other cocksucker he had ever encountered, ever glanced at on a subway platform throughout the course of his life. Such was the inclusive nature of his darkness. His talent for hate did not play favorites, his hate talent a bighearted and generous talent. *Fuck them, fuck them all,* as the slogan went. *Go ahead and rot, and as long as you're rotting, why not rot in hell?* He saw billows of black smoke chugging out of the rooftop chimney of 466, and with it his mind considered the lock removed from what was now his former front door, the old cylinder which had served so well and long no doubt tossed down the incinerator by some locksmith who would have banged his wife given half a chance, as his wife, Connie knew, was highly desirable, the lock now melting away in the furnace of what used to be his marriage, the incinerator's thick black clouds signifying love's end, and, when you thought about it, what good was a life without love?

His Rolodex of drunks included full-blown black-outs, wherein days and, in a handful of cases, weeks of the calendar got recessed for good, but more generally he browned out. Come the period following a run he could more or less piece together basic events and chronology, though he could never keep his boroughs straight. Who knew half the time if you were in Brooklyn or Queens anyway? It didn't take a drunk to produce that confusion. It was all the same nonsense out there, though the Bronx somehow remained special, while Staten Island was basically Jersey in his mind.

Some drunks he walked right into face-first with a vengeance. Others took him unawares, episodes which exceeded his daily maintenance intake, his ubiquitous hip-pocket pint of Myers's, or Bacardi 151, or any decent brand of bourbon, episodes which ended with Connie coming to on a park bench, subway car, or vestibule—or lately a hard-tiled patch of floor on Penn Station's lower level. Which disturbed him. It's one thing to wake up in some miscellaneous spot, another to find yourself retreating to the same location. Was he staking a claim? There was a word to describe such a person.

Grant's fancied itself a workingman's establishment, but fights rarely broke out. The clientele didn't possess the requisite passion for a good brawl, being largely broken men.

Whitey tended bar in rolled-up sleeves, the shirt's whiteness making the blotchy glow of Whitey's face glow harder. The bones of his hands barely distinguishable, a walrus in long pants, drinking behind the bar for free all day—isn't that right, you son of a bitch, you, Whitey?

Longshoremen, mailmen, factory workers, auto mechanics, truck drivers, the unemployable, a couple of wet-brains, a misanthropic PhD or two hiding behind what they hoped people would consider academic beards of distinction, flabbergasted occupants of Chelsea's swankier brownstones because their lives still somehow sucked despite impressive curriculum vitae and substantial earning power—all stood and drank at the bar together.

On the opposite wall lived an oak-paneled telephone booth with a door which, when unfolded and slid shut on its track, triggered illumination and ventilation from above. The phone itself sported various-sized apertures to deposit various-sized nickels, dimes, and quarters—a pair of brass knuckles reconfigured for the reception of change.

On an extended ledge of plywood a large Motorola oversaw the front room, its convex screen collecting dust at four soft right angles. The box hovered like a deus ex machina.

Connie entered with second nature. Whitey set him up with a bat and a ball. Sometimes he couldn't catch a buzz for love or money—other times half a beer put him on his ass. For the next several hours he had a difficult time forgetting himself in the manner he sought, and after countless boilermakers he rapped on the bar as a good night to Whitey, but the gesture rang hollow, and on his exit a barrage of shame captured Connie's mind.

A light rain fell. He removed his cap and shook wet from it. He watched every move he made, mocking himself with harsh viciousness for a lifetime of fraudulence. The dark beat of self-recrimination kicked in hard. No wonder she changed the lock. *Not one,* he told himself, *not one solitary clue, fucko, how to show another human being any love at all.* He walked, suffering desertion and hatred of self.

He turned right onto Ninth to not even Connie knew where, when he heard a bang. He saw Arthur and three other boys carrying pieces of two-by-four the length of baseball bats. One of the kids had smacked the hood of a parked car. They whooped and sprang like a pack of animals, and as one of them banged the wall of the bank on the corner Arthur swung his two-by-four at a garbage can and knocked it over, the trash spilling into the street. Crossing the avenue, Arthur turned and locked eyes with Connie and snapped his face away, his long hair swinging wild to catch up to his head, before the four kids rumbled toward the projects, out of sight.

Connie glanced at the clock inside the convenience store owned by Jimmy the Greek, who gave credit, on the corner of 24th. Coming up on midnight and Arthur swinging a two-by-four. Twelve years old. A school night.

He had to find a way back. Reconcile with Maureen. Be the father he himself never had. A now-or-never vibe galloped up into his consciousness. *What's it going to be?* something asked him.

He stopped for a pint at his spot on 23rd, where Herbie the liquor store clerk demonstrated his sexy style for Connie, flicking his tongue toward a case of Cutty, the tongue coming quite close to but never touching the box's cardboard.

"Do you see," Herbie said, "how I love them?"

Connie stared at him without judgment, an objective anthropologist.

Later on Greenwich Avenue, after purchasing on a

lark a quart of Olde English 800 in honor of his Frisbee grab, he took a last guzzle and threw the bottle against the wall of a Bing & Bing apartment house.

A man in a leather jacket whose pinky ring shone beneath the streetlamp yelled at Connie: "What the hell do you think you're doing?" He reached down to pick up a small dog.

Connie entered four or five bars, from which lingered various images in his mind. He stepped out onto the street at one point late into the night just as the sky was opening up, and he made a dash for the 4th Street station using the Hefty bag as a ridiculous umbrella.

On a dark and motionless CC train, the last of its kind, he opened his eyes and could not remember his own name. The cross-stitching of a wicker bench impressed itself upon his face. He stared at his own hand and wondered for a moment who it belonged to. The subway car dark and motionless; stillness abided. He reached for his bankroll, bottle, and Hefty bag, found all intact. (He had come to on the subway another time to find his pockets slit open by a straight razor.) "Who?" he said, listening for the sound of his own voice, a lost child trying to purchase anchor on himself. The ceiling fan turning slowly above him, propelled by the breeze from the open windows of the car. He scrambled internally, found a moment's peace in the fan's gentle revolutions and the shadow play it produced. He navigated into an upright position, stood, and looked out over the yard where the train had come to rest. The yard itself terrifying and pitiful, the endless expanse of track, the god-awful industry of it.

At a distance he spotted a figure, a graffiti writer

working by the light of a predawn moon, balancing on the highest rung of an orange Day-Glo ladder. Up on the balls of his feet, arm fully extended, he reached to put the final touches on his whole-car piece.

STAY HIGH, the tag read. *STAY HIGH 149.*

Connie started to weep, and with it broke the spell of alienation. He wept for his own loneliness, his fractured psyche, for all the years of longing and yearning from which he had failed to escape and continued to run. He let his pity find its release, and he wept as well with a gratitude that surprised, moved by the sight of this young man making his mark, doing his thing out here at ten minutes to five in the morning. How could you not admire the guy's desire, his raison d'être? What else but artistic compulsion could provoke such unpaid dedication at this hour? It must be so fulfilling, Connie imagined, such a life to live, that of an artist of one kind or another, so rich inside.

The echo of the ball's rattle inside the can of spray paint floated clear across the yard as the writer shook the can dry for all its worth. Connie watched him a while, before he heard another sound, that of a Metro-North train speeding toward Grand Central on a set of tracks perpendicular to the yard, and with it Connie moved to find his own way downtown.

CHAPTER TWO

HE STOOD SMOKING OUTSIDE THE OTB PARLOR on 23rd, his uniform in surprisingly decent shape given a night on the trains. He said good morning to a few people from the neighborhood heading to work before he stepped into Bickford's. Customers ate breakfast and read the paper in peace. He took a seat near the elbow of the counter.

"Morning, Con."

"How you doing, May?"

She poured him a cup. "Eating?"

"Two over easy."

"Bacon crisp?"

"Please."

The sun reflected off the Lamston's sign across the street, shot into the diner, and bounced off the mirror behind the counter, cutting Bickford's airspace in half with a smoky cylindrical beam, reminiscent of a movie house projector.

Connie generally resented food when he was on a drunk, and he knew such thoughts did not speak well of his character—what kind of troubled soul gets offended by an offer to break bread?—but other times he could eat with the best of them.

"And let me get an orange juice, and, oh yeah, some home fries if you don't mind."

"I don't mind at all, Con. With the eggs and bacon right there on the plate?"

"All right, fine, all together, one big happy family on the plate. And then, also, an English muffin."

"You got it."

He took a large gulp of water and May refilled it. "Dying of thirst here," he said, and took another gulp.

Someone seated at the counter in the corner against the wall lowered his paper. He wore glasses and was about Connie's age. He looked around, took a sip of coffee, then lifted the cigarette from his ashtray and took a pull off it. Connie and the guy looked at each other.

"Good morning," the man said.

"Good morning to you," Connie said.

"Water's important," the man said. "To flush out the internal organs."

"Are you a doctor?"

"No, but I played a doctor on *The Edge of Night* once."

"Is that right?" Connie said. "My wife's favorite."

"Thank you," the man said.

Connie considered him. "Why are you saying thank you? It's not your compliment. It's a compliment to the show. They gave you a white smock and a clipboard and a couple lines. *Nurse, when is so-and-so scheduled to be discharged?* A bit player, correct?"

"Yes. A bit player," the man conceded.

"What are you, Greek?" Connie said.

"Romanian Jew."

"Born in Romania?"

"Bucharest. Grew up in Sunnyside."

"Queens?"

"Why is that so difficult to comprehend?"

"Did you go to Sunnyside Gardens?"

"My grandfather took me to the wrestling matches."

"That's strange, don't you think, going to the wrestling matches with your grandfather?"

"In what respect?"

"Skip it," Connie said, grinning with mischief.

"You have an interesting conversational style. Did they teach you that in doorman school?"

"Good one," Connie said, "doorman school. What the hell's your name?"

They introduced themselves, and the man's name was David.

"Romanian Jew from Sunnyside by way of Bucharest. Aren't you proud. What high school?"

"Stuyvesant," David said.

"Ah," Connie said, "a brainiac."

"Something of a prodigy, yes."

"Prodigy of WHAT, you son of a bitch."

David exploded with laughter. "Mathematics."

"Is that right?"

"And music."

"Listen to you. One area of expertise isn't enough. And here you sit," Connie said, "in Bickford's with me. What a fall you've taken, what depths you've plunged."

"Speaking of which," David said, "are there any openings where you work?"

"Leaving your prodigious math and music skills aside for the moment," Connie said, "what qualifies you for the job I do?"

"More coffee, hon?" May said to David. She filled both their cups. David spooned in heavy sugar.

"Tell me the most difficult thing about being a door-man, let's start there," David said.

"All right. Take me, for example. Let's talk turkey and go into detail with specifics."

"Fine," David said, "I'm unemployed."

Connie looked for his food, lit another smoke. "You have to know people."

"Uh-huh," David said. "Know people."

"Not juggle them, because people don't like to be jug-gled. Do you like to be juggled?"

"I'm not sure I know what you mean, but for the sake of your argument, let's say I don't."

"Point is . . ." Connie said, and he thought, *What the hell is my point?* before resigning himself to cliché. "You have to be a people person." The space no longer received a direct hit of light, while the mingling aromas of break-fast foods, smoke, and coffee continued to permeate.

"Are you a people person, David?" Connie said.

"I'm talking to you."

"And why is that, do you think?"

"Teach me, Socrates."

"You're talking to me because I am the one who is a people person. If I was not me, you'd be sitting here in silence."

"And you as well. Two to tango."

"Do you have a résumé?"

"On me?"

"I'd be curious to take a look at it and see what I can do for you," Connie said, and at this they both laughed.

"Two over easy," May said, "bacon crisp, home fries, with an English muffin. Jelly, Con?"

"Please, May." To David, Connie said, "Ketchup." David passed him the bottle of Heinz.

"Do you see how I speak to people?" Connie said to David. "Personable, not obtrusive. Do you understand how to behave in such a manner?"

"Bon appétit," David said.

Connie started to dig in. "I can't remember my last meal." He went to pour some ketchup onto the side of his plate but none came out.

David said, "Hold the bottle at a forty-five-degree angle and gently tap the number 57—see it there, on the side—with the bottom of your palm."

The ketchup flowed. "Son of a sea biscuit," Connie said. "Something new every day."

Connie mixed the ketchup with the yolks of his over-easy eggs, and got some jelly involved, using the English muffin to scoop it all up. He ordered another English muffin, they were so small, really, and sat at the counter with David. They drank coffee and smoked and talked for two hours.

David's mother and father brought him and an older sister to New York when David was seven years old. A mathematics whiz as a child, he played the violin with natural élan as well. He broke his parents' hearts when he chose to pursue acting at a school called the Neighborhood Playhouse. After a while he made a little money and some small headway as an actor. He married a beautiful young woman he met at the Playhouse who came from theatrical aristocracy and had family money. David told Connie he used to live in an apartment house where Connie himself might have worked, on 82nd and Park, and that it all came tumbling down six months ago.

"Where do you live now?" Connie said.

"In a rooming house around the corner."

"Anything available?"

"You serious?"

"Got kicked out," Connie said, holding up the Hefty bag. "I slept on the subway last night, a bench the night before."

"I'm on welfare," David said.

"I grew up on welfare."

"What is this, a competition?"

"Are you getting food stamps?"

"Should I?"

"My guess is you're going to be up and running better than before. You got too much to offer with all that so-called talent you claim to possess."

"True."

"Tell me about this rooming house."

"Better yet," David said, "I'll show it to you. I think she might have something."

Connie grabbed David's check.

"No," David said.

"Relax. Who is she?"

"Mrs. Cook, the manager. And if I say you're a friend of mine, well, you can imagine."

They left Bickford's and walked around the corner on a beautiful spring morning in Chelsea. The rooming house, on 22nd between Eighth and Ninth, didn't look bad, if a bit faded, with only the strange variety of window dressings suggesting a lack of internal cohesion.

Connie followed David into the vestibule. Just inside

on the left was a door which David knocked on. They waited a good while before it slowly opened.

"Mrs. Cook."

"Oh, hello, David," an old lady said.

"Mrs. Cook, this is my friend Connie, he's a doorman as you can tell, and he's looking for a room."

"Nice to meet you," Connie said.

"Are you a doorman?" Mrs. Cook said.

"Yes, yes I am," Connie replied with false modesty.

"Well," David said, "I'll leave you two alone," starting for the staircase. "I'm ready for my midmorning nap." He stopped, came back, and said to them both, "What's nice about this house is that it's very *quiet.*"

"Good," Connie said, "I like quiet."

David shook Connie's hand. "Thank you for breakfast," he said, and, "He's a good man, Mrs. Cook."

She looked at Connie, letting her eyes scan him head to foot. "Come in." She stood back and opened her door. Connie entered the front room, which smelled of old lady. "Sit down if you like."

He took a seat in a saggy chair, the room too darkly curtained for the brilliant day. He made a show of removing his doorman's cap and holding it in his hands: you don't wear your cap in front of a lady.

Mrs. Cook disappeared through a curtain as Connie continued to feign behavior. He watched himself act the innocent, holding his cap as if a simple immigrant who never had a sexual thought in his life, instead of the deranged American deviant he knew himself to be. Because if Mrs. Cook apprehended the truth concerning that which persisted in Connie's wretched heart and mind, how could she in good conscience offer him a room? She returned with some Pepperidge Farm cookies fanned out on a tray.

"Would you like a cookie?"

"I'd love a cookie."

Mrs. Cook moved slow, spoke slow, and Connie wanted to strangle her. She might have been in her eighties—but you don't ask a woman her age. Through the room's shadows Connie spotted a portrait of John's father on the wall, the man gone ten-plus years. It looked as if the photograph had been retouched with some cheap colorization: a little rouge had been applied to the assassinated president's cheeks, with a faint dab of lipstick.

Mrs. Cook placed the tray of cookies between them on the coffee table, and took a seat across from Connie. "David told me you were a nice man," she said.

"That's nice of him."

"And you're a doorman."

"Yes," Connie said, modestly touching the lapel of his uniform.

"Could your supervisor provide a reference?"

"Sure, Mr. Mezzola. No problem. Would it be possible," Connie ventured, "to move in today?"

"I don't see why not," Mrs. Cook said, "but you haven't seen the room yet. Let me get the key."

"I'm sure it's lovely," Connie said, and wondered who just said *that*. He smiled at Mrs. Cook, eager to have the question of shelter resolved, when he flashed on the bedroom he shared with Maureen, bringing forth the room's scent as well, of love and home and the small touches of comfort his wife attempted to provide—but no, he would not miss the mirror of her eyes reflecting the failure of his life back at him.

He let Mrs. Cook lead him up the staircase. She took one step at a time. Connie noticed her left shoe had an orthopedic lift, and the sight of it helped to temper his impatience.

"I hope I brought the right key with me," she said.

"Me too," Connie chuckled, and again he thought, *Why am I being such a phony? It's just a room in a rooming house.* Mrs. Cook, he realized, reminded him of his mother, if only in that she was an older Irish-American woman.

Connie had done a dance for his mother his entire life, until he started to avoid her altogether, and when she died he felt enormous relief, which he felt inclined to keep hidden. *Thank God*, he had thought. *Finally. Let her be dead already. About fucking time.* These sentiments became part of the guilt cloud under which he roamed.

How did I come to hate my mother? he wondered. *Do a lot of people hate their mothers?* Did he really hate his mother? Was it more common than he suspected? *My sainted mother. With her one tattered housecoat, always talking about what a saint her own mother was, and therefore, what, I should talk about what a saint you are?*

Connie spotted a black-haired, blue-eyed woman at the top of the stairs. Beautiful and disturbed, in a sexy way, to Connie. Black and blue, a rare steak. Mrs. Cook didn't see her, but Connie did, and when he locked eyes with the woman she moved out of view, and Connie heard a door shut on the floor.

Mrs. Cook fumbled with the key but managed to open a door at the top of stairs.

"Nice and bright," Connie said.

"It might be a little noisy in the front."

"I was raised on noise's knee."

"I can find you a pair of clean sheets and, let's see, a pillowcase, and a blanket or two, unless you have your own linen."

"No, I could use some linen, thank you," and this he said in a voice closer to his own.

Mrs. Cook said the room cost $155 a month, Con Ed included. It was May 15, so she said, "Let's say seventy dollars for the month of May."

Connie told her he would give her the money tomorrow if that was all right, and Mrs. Cook said it wouldn't be a problem.

"It's a very easygoing house," she said. "And I have a feeling you're a decent man." She placed the key to the room flat in the palm of Connie's hand, and started back downstairs.

"Oh, would you like a few towels?" she called.

"Yes please."

He turned, looked at the room. The ceiling was high and the window was large, its scale a nod to former grandeur, and Connie imagined the house prior to its getting chopped into cubicles, seeing its bearded sea-captain patriarch surrounded by a half-dozen rosy-cheeked children clamoring for his attention after his return from a long voyage.

A rush of exhaustion hit him. He sat on the room's naked mattress, smaller than a twin, closer to the size of a cot. He took off his cap, removed his shoes. He bent over, head in hands, and said a quick prayer to some god he did not believe in, not really, a word of thanks for a place to sleep. "Thank you, Lord," Connie said, "for this room, for this spring day."

He went to the window and shucked it open. A lovely tree-lined block, what it was. And there, where a branch the height of Connie's window met the trunk of a tree, a nest. Connie watched one bird bouncing. He saw two chicks pop into view. Sure enough, here came another bird, and this one's got something in its mouth. Beak-to-beak they eat. Connie watched the chicks get fed and found it too marvelous for words.

If a bird knows how to live. If a bird can make a nest.

He had learned, he feared, from his mother how not to get involved in the world or its people in any intimate way. *What a terribly sad thing. My poor mother. To wind up with a man like Pete Cullen, you have to be sick, no?* Such a locked-down life, and Connie picked up on it, the art of isolation. In the middle of some party, surrounded by people who only wanted to love and care for you, and there you stood behind the wall of your apartness, there but not there.

People along the way had showed Connie love. His sense of humor and other positive traits did not spring from the head of Zeus after all, but finally he could not stand people looking to be in his life in any authentic way.

He watched the birds with a smile, and the people walking down the block. He daintily produced his work schedule, and realized it was a Wednesday. He had the day off.

Out in the hallway a door opened and closed. Connie pushed away from the window and went to his room's threshold. The woman with the black hair and blue eyes came into view from the far side of the floor.

"Hello," Connie said.

The woman said, "Hello," moving toward the staircase, and Connie said, "What's your name?"

"Susan," she said.

"I'm Connie. Do you live here?"

"I do. Did you just move in?"

"Got the key from Mrs. Cook two seconds ago."

"Welcome to our humble abode."

"Thank you," Connie said.

They smiled at one another, then Susan turned down the staircase.

Connie watched her descend, and without looking back she said, "I like your socks, by the way."

A pair of green argyles adorned Connie's feet. And he knew with Susan's compliment the possibility of them making love existed. It's how his mind worked. What's more, he oftentimes proved himself correct in these matters. Connie became instantly taken with this woman named Susan, and since they now lived together, so to speak, it only made sense they should get to know one another in that special way.

He closed the door. The thought of trekking down to Mrs. Cook's for linen seemed too much. *Let me just lie down here a minute*, he thought. The naked mattress cradled his body decently enough, before he sat up with a sudden force of will to remove his jacket, shirt, and pants. He went to the window, closed it most of the way, returned to the bed, and curled up on his right side.

His mother always told him to sleep on his right side. When he coughed his head off at night she'd appear in the doorway of the bedroom he shared with Danny and Patrick and Edward. His mother would say, *Who's coughing?*

Con, his brothers would say.

Turn on your right side, his mother would say, and disappear.

He lay down and, tired as he was, his mind ran. He did the thing he read about: he stepped onto an imaginary escalator heading south, an escalator of wooden steps with large spaces between its teeth, like the ones in Gimbels. Only this, an infinite escalator, traveling to forever. Slowly, slowly he descended, and his mind eased up, unhinged itself from the workaday world, the escalator's gentle, steady movement gliding his body down, down, and Connie thought, *I'm falling asleep*, when he suddenly twitched from an incident in an already-forgotten dream, and it stirred him back to the texture of his naked mattress. He readjusted his body, curled tight onto his right side, like a fetus in the womb of the world, a grown man yet unborn, and stepped onto the escalator in his mind.

Four hours later he woke to a knock at the door.

"My mother likes you."

"Does she?"

"Heard her on the phone."

"Surprised."

"What you did to the lobby floor. *Could get you a job across the street*, she said"—meaning the Met—"*restoring works of art*."

"Hardly says boo to me."

"It's kind of how she is sometimes, Con. She's been through a lot."

"I know she has, John."

"Check."

"Check how check?"

"My rook. *And* my bishop."

"What's that?"

"A bowl of hashish. Your Zippo needs more lighter fluid."

"Nah, it's the flint gone bad."

He rolled onto his back and through the window's upper-left pane saw a patch of blue with hints of pink in the northwestern sky of Manhattan.

"Who's there?"

"Did I wake you?" David said from the hall.

"No—I mean . . . yes," Connie said, thick with sleep.

"One flight up," David said, "number seven."

Connie's extended nap brought access to a simple appreciation for this stopgap roof over his head. He went into the shared bathroom on the floor. He knew Susan had a connection to it. It smelled feminine. The shower curtain displayed frogs on rocks, big toothy grins on their froggy-but-also-human faces. He went up the off-kilter staircase through a wispy cloud of Lysol and knocked on seven.

"Get some shut-eye?"

"Like a baby."

David sat with a man about fifty years old.

"This is Justin, he's in the room next door."

Justin wore a corduroy blazer and khakis, and looked the part of a disheveled intellect. Connie's first thought about him was, *He's flattering us with his presence*, but then the way Justin tapped his cigarette at the ashtray suggested a genuine kindness.

"Sit."

Connie sat next to David on the bed, with Justin facing them in the room's chair: a hub of six knees knocking.

"Cozy," he said.

"That it is, that it is," David said. "What can you do? We're a close-knit family. We've all come down a peg."

"Or two," Justin said.

Connie lit up and they sat there smoking. David jarred the window as open as the layered coats of paint permitted.

"Connie moved in this morning. He's a doorman."

"Welcome," Justin said.

"Thank you. How long you been here?"

"Thanksgiving," Justin said.

"And what about yourself?" Connie said to David.

"Christmas."

"Holidays are a time of change," Justin said.

"Shit goes down come the holidays," David said.

"Lives collapse, families dissolve before perfectly cooked hams and turkeys," Justin said.

"What about me?" Connie said. "I need a holiday to mark my move into Mrs. Cook's rooming house, which, by the way, did I thank you, David, sufficiently?"

"No, you did not."

"Sunday is Mother's Day," Justin said.

"Fuck Mother's Day," Connie said.

"Said the bishop to the queen," Justin said, pursing his lips slightly.

"Does Mrs. Cook have children?" David wondered.

"She set out a tray of Pepperidge Farm cookies on my behalf," Connie said.

"Something out of Tennessee Williams," Justin said.

"Susan likes the theater," David said.

"Wait now," Connie said. "Hold on a second."

"She's on your floor," Justin said, "room five."

"Right below me," David said. "I wish we had a woman on our floor."

"She complimented my socks," Connie said.

"I leave the bathroom as I find it," Justin said.

"She's a beauty," Connie said.

"She has her charms," David said. "A beauty she's not."

"She's *my* beauty. Tell me about her in great detail."

Susan worked as a proofreader and copy editor through a temp agency Justin had referred her to. She smoked Sherman cigarettes, the sweet brown filterless ones. Her people were from Oklahoma but she grew up outside DC. She had two older brothers, one of whom ran a small hotel in Florida. The other, a professor, lived with his family in the high desert east of San Diego. Every once in a while a mouthwatering aroma escaped her door. A miracle, they concurred, to produce such gastronomical wonders on a rooming house hot plate. David said Susan moved in on the Fourth of July and they laughed.

"Has she had, our Susan, any gentlemen callers?" Justin asked.

"None that I'm aware of," David said.

"Does she like men," Justin said, "or does she hate men?"

"That she was quite interested in me I can state without equivocation," David said.

A short bark of astonishment escaped Connie.

"I could have had her," David said, "no question, but I'm taking a year off."

"A year off?" Connie said.

"Not getting involved with anyone for a year."

"I don't know what the hell you're talking about," Connie said. "I'm not taking any time off. She paid me an unsolicited compliment on my argyle socks, from which I envision a lovemaking session in our very near future."

"Forgive me, I say it to spare you, but the woman liked your *socks*."

"Exactly," Connie said. "A woman doesn't say things like *I like your socks* for no reason. Ah, David," Connie said, "you'll learn," and they laughed some more.

To a barely audible knock David said, "Come in, Mrs. Cook."

Connie reached for the knob. The old lady held a small stack of folded laundry in her arms.

"Thank you, Mrs. Cook. What do I owe you?"

"Seventy-five cents. I ran out of fabric softener, so I deducted a quarter."

"They feel plenty soft," David said, and placed the clothes on top of the dresser.

Connie followed Mrs. Cook downstairs for linen. He returned to his room and made his bed before dumping the contents of the Hefty bag onto it. Next to a small sink, a hot plate sat atop a half-pint fridge. Connie emptied his pockets—money, wallet, smokes, change, keys—into the chipped six-inch skillet on the plate. The room's furnishings suggested a deeply ingrained futility in the late-afternoon light, like pieces in a museum honoring the history of sad people. He started to undress, hanging his uniform and other clothes in the closet. Maureen had tossed his favorite items into the bag, things she knew he preferred, more evidence of a still-caring touch, which Connie took as a hopeful sign for the survival of their marriage.

For Connie, a hot shower with strong water pressure described a key amenity of heaven. He stood in the tub and let it burn down on him. He scoured his body with a soapy washcloth, performing the whole shebang of personal care and hygiene. He let his toiletry products mingle with the toiletry products of, he felt sure, Susan, there on the shower's convenient chest-high window ledge. It crossed his mind to masturbate but he didn't want to indiscriminately discard his chi like that. There's a place in the world for a good jerk, but a steady diet of it gets played out. Besides, he wanted to save himself for Susan, bring the entire catalog of his lust, the full brunt of his desire, directly to her this very night. *I'll ravish her in a way she has never been ravished before*, he thought, not without a fair amount of sexual self-importance. Now that they shared the same bathroom he felt an intimacy had established itself, and that in some essential way he already practically possessed her, their carnal connection a done deal. These were his thoughts, relayed from self to self, when he nicked himself, and a spot of red appeared at his jaw and brought him back to where he stood, naked before the bathroom mirror, the cap of his small circumcised dick at rest against the chilly porcelain rim of the sink basin. He chuckled at the nature of his own fantastical mind and continued to shave.

He waited outside the rooming house in his favorite button-down sweater, leaning against the fin of a car in a holdover pose from teenage times, smoking. People headed home up and down the block. New York bloomed through its filth and decay and somewhere in the city Andy Warhol was saying yes to money.

He waited not ten minutes. Something in him knew she would appear. He believed he summoned her, evoked her presence, and here she came, carrying a bag of groceries from International Supermarket, offering a smile.

"I knew I'd see you," Connie said.

"Did you?" Susan said.

"Like what they call a karma thing, maybe, synchronicity or something. I said, *She's going to show any second.*"

"Funny, my schedule's off today."

"I wanted to ask you something," Connie said.

"Yes?"

"Would you like to take a walk downtown and have dinner tonight . . . Can I buy you dinner?"

"Tonight?"

"If it's okay with you."

A moment's silence, as if someone, somewhere, was counting to three.

"That would be nice," Susan said.

"Beautiful."

"Can you give me a few minutes?"

She came down in a dress, a casual one, swapping out her sneakers for a pair of sandals. Also, she had applied a little makeup around the eyes, and some lipstick.

"You look terrific."

"Thank you," she said, and what was nice, it seemed to Connie, was her sincerity. She appreciated the compliment, and with it he knew they might very well sleep together if he could manage not to sabotage the situation.

They walked down Ninth Avenue and Connie touched her, a brief hand at the wrist to switch positions on the sidewalk. He wanted to walk closest to the street, in the event a truck jumped the curb, in which case he could push Susan to safety and die a heroic death. When he touched her, Susan didn't flinch, and what Connie truly thought was, *I'm in*.

"You smell good," he said.

"Thank you."

"Thank you for going out with me."

"Thank you for inviting me."

"All right, enough!" Connie cried out, startling passersby, and Susan laughed a good one from her belly. "No more thank yous," he said. "Enough with the heartfelt appreciation. All this predictable well-mannered nonsense. *Thank you this, thank you that*. If I hear one more, one more thank you . . ." Connie held her for a moment in the palm of his hand. "Seriously though," he said.

Susan, with coy trepidation, said: "Yes?"

"Do you like how I walk, by the way, how I take each step in stride?" He made a grand sweeping gesture with his arm as they headed south together.

"Yes," Susan said, "you're quite accomplished."

The talk was small, subservient to the walk. Susan was working on a book project for McGraw-Hill about woodworking—a snooze, but hey, it paid the rent. Connie flew over his personal circumstances without emotion, spoke of his kids and troubled marriage, saying that although he had just separated, things had been rocky for ages, and he tied the subject up with a whattayagonnado shrug of the shoulders.

"Would you like to take a look at the river?"

They walked beneath the abandoned West Side Highway and found an abandoned pier, it being a time of great abandonment. The scene had *tetanus shot* written all over it. Connie extended his hand to help Susan negotiate the broken bottles, nails, and uneven planks. She reached for him, her palm just a little moist with nerves—not clammy, not some clinical disorder like what they said Connie's father had before he turned on the oven. The note written on the back of a letter from Bellevue. As a nine-year-old the irony was not lost on Connie, to write your suicide note on the back of a notice from Bellevue confirming your appointment as regards your nervous disorder.

They stood at the pier's end, the river serene if you didn't look straight down into the water where terrible filth floated, nasty man-made pollution banging up against itself, trying to get away from itself. The poor Hudson.

"This is nice," Susan said, good sport.

"Have you been to Hoboken?"

"No."

"We should go one day, take the tubes, get some steamers at the Clamhouse. Do you like seafood?"

"I can't think of any food I don't much like."

He studied her profile as she studied the water. By no means overweight, nor was she frail. She had good height for a woman, not small-boned but well-proportioned, and something vaguely tragic about her look as well. Connie couldn't put a finger on it, yet he was drawn to her because *like attracts like*, they say. The space between her nose and mouth turned him on. A woman like this, in a rooming house: how sad is that?

They walked south and east, cutting through the Village.

"I prefer 4th to Bleecker for some reason," Connie said, but the *for some reason* part was disingenuous: he got his ass kicked badly on Bleecker Street when he was nineteen. Some kid attacked him, sly-rapped him dead in his face, a blunt object to the bridge of his nose, blinding him. Connie swung a few times in pathetic defense, listening to vicious laughter. He tried to flee onto Carmine Street, stumbled in the black snow on the steps to Our Lady of Pompeii, while the kid continued to kick and punch. A performance for his peers, Connie figured. The beating itself nothing in light of the emotional aftereffects, a result of the attack's randomness, the entropic nature of the violence forever altering his take on the world below the level of consciousness. The mob's laughter. Did the guy say, *Watch this*, before striking the first blow, or did Connie layer the line in during countless mental replays? He limped around like an old raccoon with two severely blackened eyes for a month, his olfactory connection to the world permanently dampened, one more loss he had yet to mourn.

They decided on Chinatown. They saw a place on the Bowery with a photograph of Muhammad Ali taped in a slapdash fashion to its window and entered on a lark.

Connie used a fork, Susan chopsticks. She ate without pretension, nothing birdlike about it, and Connie knew she was good in bed. They drank tea and Coca-Cola, ate soup and dumplings and noodles, a chicken dish and a pork dish with sautéed vegetables. They could see the blinking lights of the Manhattan Bridge from their table. They smoked and watched the waiters work. One very tall waiter towered over his comrades, holding plates of food high above his head, letting them swoop down onto tables. Customers applauded him, and Connie spotted another waiter in the shadows grimacing with universal envy.

They hailed a Checker cab and Connie asked the driver if he could take the FDR.

"A lot of river tonight," Susan said.

They turned and took in the sight of the bridges receding out the rear window.

"Thank you," Susan said, and she offered him a soft kiss on the lips.

Connie unfolded the jump seat facing her and hopped onto it. He pulled her gently by the legs toward him, and they started to make out.

Connie followed her up the rooming house staircase.

"There's a bottle in my room."

"Get it," she said.

Susan produced two glasses on a table and placed them in front of Connie. She kissed him and quietly left. *To use the bathroom*, Connie thought. That visit women often make before sex. He hummed with anticipation, poured some bourbon. He glanced out the window, into the backyards, saw a dilapidated bicycle built for two chained to a fence.

Susan returned, gently closed the door. She sat next to Connie on the bed and he offered her a drink.

He looked at her, and he didn't know why, but his eyes got glassy. He took a swallow of booze and said, "Who are you?"

"Who am I?"

"Proofreader . . . small college in Vermont . . . good with a hot plate, so they say. Two brothers . . . father something called an economist . . . mother a librarian."

"Are you getting philosophical with me?" Susan said.

A vacuum of silence suddenly filled the space.

"Quiet in the back," he said.

He reached for her. They adjusted their bodies on the bed, the better to kiss. He took her jaw in hand and lined her face up to appropriate the full benefit of her mouth. She reached for his dick, found it, and made a noise as he continued to kiss her. He broke from her, got up, and took his pants off.

"I need to unrestrict my balls," he said.

Susan laughed and reached to shut off the lamp. The room lit now by dirty moonlight.

"Can people hear?" he whispered.

"Who cares?" She stood up, shook her sandals off, let the dress fall from her body. Connie kissed her stomach, held her by the back of her thighs.

"Something about you," he said. He sat on the room's chair. "Straddle me, would you?" And she did. "You're so light. The weight of you."

"Am I?"

He started to kiss her nipples, first with some dry, getting-acquainted kisses, simple and slow, before folding in some tongue and saliva.

"Are they sensitive?"

"Yes," she said earnestly. She made little sex noises which were genuine, and her breath caught, as Connie continued to kiss and suck.

He had been with women who felt compelled to act turned on when Connie sensed they were not turned on, and it threw him. He himself liked sex quite a bit, when not completely shame-scalded by it. He'd been on the make his whole life. Others, it seemed, were more successful in transmuting their sex drive, going on to achieve a full platter of accomplishments: careers, country homes, pilot licenses, PTA participation, qualifying for Olympic teams, you name it. There was so much to tackle, so much to learn, and be, and do, when you weren't looking to get laid round the clock. Connie's lifelong sexuality had carried with it a sorrowful burden, and the tyranny of compulsion as well.

Oddly, given its obsessive prominence in his life, he had never made a serious study of it. It essentially remained a mystery to him, a woman's vagina, which was maybe part of its appeal. He did his best to help women come, he took natural pleasure in it, he loved the taste and smell of pussy, it turned him on to watch a woman's face when she came, yet the whole business simultaneously made him uptight.

He himself only came once as a rule, during what he assumed would be quantified as a stand-alone lovemaking session. Growing up, shooting the shit with the fellas over a game of pool, or anywhere else guys who bragged about how many times they came during a described blow-by-blow fuck-fest congregated, he personally never understood coming more than once. After he came once he was done, he had no interest in coming twice. The French had a phrase for what he felt after his lonely little orgasm. And since he knew he was done once he came once, he felt beholden to his partner that she come before he come, if she were going to come at all. Soon after penetration there arrived a moment, generally within those first eighteen or twenty seconds, when he had to stay mindful. *Wait, wait a minute now*, he'd say, *hold tight*, and he did something he learned as a kid: he thought about his dead aunt Loretta, who represented in Connie's mind all things unhorny, unsexy, and anticlimactic, the vision of Aunt Loretta serving to distract the blood-rush to his dick for the necessary split-second in which he might manage to circumvent the onslaught of orgasm. He would lie on top of his partner, stock-still in the eye of a premature ejaculatory storm, until the threat moved on. After which he could resume for what he thought would be considered a decent stretch.

He liked to delay penetration, and he enjoyed kissing, and the use of his hands, and sixty-nine-ing he found quite gratifying as well, plus he could eat a woman's ass for an hour if it be her pleasure. He enjoyed all this and more, and it filled him with a white-hot shame.

He kissed and licked Susan's nipples which sat in front of his face. It was good stuff, and Susan for her part had a difficult time sitting still on his lap. He liked her agitation and periodically kissed her deeply. He alternated from nipples to mouth, and it seemed to be working out okay. He made a jumping-type move out of the chair, to quickly position his hand between her legs. The softness of skin inside her thigh: tender is the flesh. The smell of her made him hard as a rock. She started to moan and groan. He reached for her vagina, grabbed it with audacity, her box his possession to do with what he wished for, let's say, the next six minutes if they were both lucky.

"I can't wait to get the taste of your sweet pussy in my mouth, if it's all right to say so," Connie said.

She got up and went to the bed and scooched her body against the wall, to make room for Connie. They pressed together. To feel a connection, to be close to one another, their legs intertwined, her wetness, how wrong is that?

Sometimes he feared his lovemaking technique was a little by-the-book. Usually he liked to kiss for a while, before he started in on the nipples, combined with deep tongue kissing. Then, after a time, cunnilingus would go down.

"Would you hold it open for me?" Connie said, and Susan spread the lips of her vagina, otherwise known as the *labia*, he believed. He admired her fleshy drapery, took in a deep whiff of its delicious pungency, started to ever so gently kiss and lick. He snorted and made a physical adjustment to his body on the bed and said, "I need to orientate myself."

Susan chuckled and said, "Would you like a compass?" and they both laughed, and it was good laughter, it made the sex relaxed and easy and fun. "A sextant?" she said, more to herself, a husk in her voice. "My clit is true north," she said, and with helpful instruction which Connie gratefully accepted, she came without too much fanfare. Her body tensed and shook, and she pushed Connie's mouth away from her, grabbed him by the wrist to stop his hand.

Connie looked confused, his face red and sweating. "Is it all right?" he said. She pulled him toward her, wrapped her arms around him. She reached for his dick, gave it a confident pump. He liked the way she held it. He had a five-point-two-five-inch erection, super firm, the tip of it swollen like a small bruised plum. She brought her other hand to her mouth, gave her palm a thorough lick, and with this wet hand cupped his balls. She went down on him, started to suck his dick with wonderful delight and eagerness, and what a singular pleasure to have a woman suck your dick who really, you could tell, wanted to.

"Careful, careful," Connie said, "don't forget I want to fuck you," as if mentioning one more item on their to-do list.

"Lie back," she said, and Connie obeyed, and never letting go of him, she straddled and slid down onto him. She rose up, getting into a position of maximum fuckability, gripping the wall behind Connie's head.

"Fuck me," he said, and Susan started to do so. He watched her face, older now in the moonlight, and from this angle of body and light he knew she had had a baby from the faint trace of stretch marks around her breasts and belly, knew also this baby-having was part of the tragic sorrow she carried in her heart and somehow informed her presence in the rooming house, and he reached to kiss her, and Susan rose up again and Connie stayed stock-still and let her gain greater purchase.

"Give me your cock," she said over and over, louder, and she started to scream, and she crescendoed, went and came full out, and Connie came too, came with her, but it was nothing compared to how she came, Susan gone altogether, crying out with abandonment. Her juices flowed from her, flooding Connie's genitalia, his balls flooding wet and warm. She collapsed onto him, her cries of pleasure transforming into tears. She wept, and Connie held her, her body rocking and sobbing, her belly jiggling against his.

"Ow," she said, and shook out a cramping leg. She pushed away to look at him, smiled, and held his head. Connie brushed the hair from her face, kissed her eyebrows. She scooted down, rested herself against him, and together they fell asleep for fifteen minutes.

"How old were you?"

"Me? Fifteen. Yeah. Me and my wife. Fifteen both." Connie shuffled the cards. "But you don't have to worry about that stuff."

"Huh?"

"I'm saying you got time for all that. No rush."

"Already been laid," John said.

"*Already* been laid?"

"Like, last year."

"Last year. You're thirteen. Last year you were *twelve*."

"So?" John laughed.

"Hell you getting laid at twelve years old for?"

"What am I supposed to do, Con? They throw themselves at me." They laughed. "I know. Because of my name. Mostly. Probably."

"No. Not just your name. You're a good-looking kid with a good personality. All right," Connie said. "Now let me tell you something. And this is all I have to say on the subject. You know what an aphrodisiac is?"

"Makes you more horny."

"Correct. Even *more* horny, imagine that, if such a thing were possible. And do you know what the greatest aphrodisiac is?"

"The greatest?"

"The greatest aphrodisiac . . . is when you really *like* somebody. To be really fond of somebody. You want to have great sex? Find somebody you totally dig. I mean, from the ground up. Somebody you just like talking to, you know. Trust me—the main ingredient. And that's all I have to say on the matter."

"I hear you, Con."

In his attempt to say something helpful and paternal, Connie, given his own track record in the realm of sex and love, felt like a hypocrite, yet he also believed what he said to be true.

* * *

He looked out onto 22nd Street, his body shrouded in a Zen-like, after-lovemaking calm. And yet. A strangeness remained, a vague dread persisted. He smoked and drank and his future whispered vexations. The stillness of the night and his mind clamored. Ever so. His heart a discordant murmur all the days of his life. An achy muscle or two from the time with Susan, and yesterday's pursuit of the Frisbee, the pain not a bad pain, serving to ground him.

After they awoke and Susan invited him to leave, he took himself and the bottle back to his room. He studied the front parlor of a brownstone across the street, unsure if he heard a ringing telephone, when a soft knock came.

"I saw your light on," David said.

"I didn't see you coming."

"The light beneath your door. I was upstairs."

"Want a drink?"

"No thank you—I have a job interview tomorrow."

"For what?"

"Acting teacher."

"Is that right, acting teacher? I can see that," Connie said.

David sat on the bed and watched him take a swallow of bourbon. "Forgive me," David said. He smiled and rubbed his face. "But you might not know . . . given your recent arrival."

"Spit it out."

"These walls," David said, "are like tissue," and let himself expel laughter.

"I'm not sure it happened, if that makes any sense."

"Oh, it happened," David said, "it happened."

They walked the midnight streets at David's suggestion, theirs a quick and trustworthy connection. David expounded on the mythology of his life, his rise and fall. The pressure-cooker expectations cast upon him by his parents. His talent for all things musical and mathematical. The bullying from the Irish boys in Sunnyside, running to and from his building, hugging his violin. His boredom at elementary school, these American children so entirely slow. He picked up the English language like a glass of water and watched himself soar. He studied and nailed the entrance exam to Stuyvesant High School. He flourished there, found himself popular, a boy taller than most and, would you believe it, he could dance. Precocious, bespectacled, and funny, and the girls ate it up.

They headed east, passing Madison Square Park, which had been commandeered as a base by drug addicts and the homeless. Connie let him talk. From eleven on he waited tables, David and his sister, alongside their mother and father, the family waiting tables, a Romanian joint on 46th Street, the children cracking the books in a back booth when it got slow. Working, studying, playing the violin in the All-City band, the final concert performed at Carnegie Hall a brief eight years after the jet wheels touched American soil.

"Not a solo performance," Connie ribbed.

"First chair—have you played Carnegie Hall?"

They made a left onto Third Avenue. David told of the moment he learned what he wanted to do with his life, a subtle epiphany in an acting class at the Playhouse, and the subsequent breaking of his parents' hearts, though maybe his father's heart broke slightly less, with the announcement of his plans to become a—

"*What?* What did he say?" his mother said.

"An actor," David said.

"Is he crazy?" his mother said to his father.

"I have found my calling," David said, standing before them like Edwin Booth on the kitchen's cracked linoleum. "Be happy for me, why don't you?"

David's father reached for David's throat. His mother gripped the back of a chair lest she collapse.

"The tables we have waited on," she wailed.

"I've waited on tables too," David cried.

He had rejected a full musical scholarship to Julliard, in order to attend the Neighborhood Playhouse.

"Where you will have to pay!" his mother said. "Are you stupid? Are you trying to drive us crazy? All right, if not music, do business like your sister. But to put paint on your face, some hyena, for people to laugh at you? Please, David. Please. Consider us," she beseeched in Romanian. "I beg you, consider us." It sounded like Latin, but with strong Jewish roots accenting the more desperate syllables.

David led Connie into a place called the Starlit Diner on 36th and Third. A waiter shook David's hand and sat them at a rather large table in the back.

David remained steadfast in his desire, and henceforth his parents withheld their love, the mother more so, their words clipped with disappointment, a frugality of tone. The passive-aggressive silences on the overseas phone calls to this day. He had broken the family contract and got branded a blood traitor, the emotional abbreviation from his parents for years on end taking a toll. But such was the power of his calling to the stage. He wanted to act, period, cost what it may—even family. David's sister earned an MBA and JD from Penn State, followed by enormous real estate success, and the family returned to Romania.

"They left me here," David said.

"God almighty," Connie said. "Can you pass the syrup?"

Connie ordered what the menu called a Farmer's Boy Special, two breakfasts rolled into one: pancakes and eggs, toast and butter, bacon and sausage. The waiter kept the coffee coming.

David cited the names of Playhouse alumni to his parents, which to his mother meant nothing, but David caught the spark in his father's eye at the mention of certain names, this same father who had taken David as a child to all the old cinema houses of Bucharest, and later Greenwich Village.

"Father, please," David said, "explain it to Mother."

The movies were their special time, father and son. David's sister, mother-bound, did not attend these outings.

"You know, Father, why I need to pursue this. You know. Please. I know you know."

They would walk together hand in hand, discussing the just-seen pictures, David a precocious six-year-old, asking so many questions of his father on their way home. The father carrying figs for them in a small brown bag in the pocket of his long black overcoat.

The father torn between wife and son. He looked from one to the other, David's future hanging in the balance, not to mention the love of the parents for each other, and their love for David himself. The look in his mother's eyes.

You should right now spit in my face, because that's what you've done. That stupid 7 train, seven days a week, that lousy restaurant, in a language that sounded like the voice of God.

David ordered a black-and-white milkshake and Connie told the waiter to put it on his ticket. One forty-five a.m. on a nothing weeknight and the Starlit was jumping. The city's mentally ill spilled out into the mix, and Connie spotted one such man heading straight to the bathroom, a scuffed briefcase in hand, the man attempting to look industrious, Connie realizing the man was jobless and homeless, the thread of his life having snapped a good ways back.

"And then I met the woman who was to become my wife, my first class at the Playhouse, summer of '61," David said.

"The one from theater royalty?"

"Turns out she couldn't act, not a lick, so she bowed out with grace, and at the moment she's interning at Lenox Hill in geriatrics. So beautiful, if you saw her."

David wrapped up his life's story: the start of his career, some early soap-opera work, his marriage, a string of B movies he refused to divulge the names of due to a previous run of obesity, his divorce.

After some quiet, when Connie had cleaned his plate, he sat back, lit a cigarette, and said, "I don't get it. There's a gap in your story."

Fourteen people stormed into the rear of the diner, laughing, addressing David, slapping him on the back, fourteen men and women haranguing him about his whereabouts.

"Who spoke?" David asked.

"Guy named Louie from Pax," somebody said.

"Powerful," another said. "Powerful qualification."

A guy looked at Connie and said, "What do you got here, a wet one?" and Connie laughed, embarrassed and confused. There were too many of them, they talked all at once and their eyes shone funny, this gang of fourteen bombing their way into the back of the Starlit. They surrounded Connie and David at the table, the crowd running the gamut from old-man-banker-in-a-suit to young-slut-in-a-minidress, the group as a whole defying strata altogether, there in the back of the Starlit.

They had come from a midnight AA meeting at the Moravian Church on 30th Street and Lexington Avenue. Some sober for days, some others, decades. Some ordered big, some just coffee. They talked all at once, telling pope jokes and rabbi jokes, jokes about all kinds of animals, about people, places, and things walking into bars.

A fountain pen walks into a bar.

Half of a horse's ass walks into a bar.

Down the table Connie heard, "I wanted to drink so bad I thought my face was going to explode." He exchanged looks with David through the din.

"What's up?" Connie said.

"Nothing. I know them."

"Yeah, I put that much together."

"Fuck a higher power," somebody said, "I just don't want to wet the bed anymore."

Connie grabbed his head as if his foxhole had taken a direct mortar hit.

"Sexually," another guy said, "I don't know if I'm coming or going," and the guy across from him said, "You're in the right place," and this brought more laughter.

Next to Connie a guy with thick eyeglasses whose leg

would not stop bouncing beneath the table said, "How many days you got?"

Connie snatched at his check, sprang from his chair.

He felt disembodied on his way back to the rooming house, moving through the streets under some inarticulate threat. *Two nuns a priest and a rabbi walk into a bar.* Connie didn't like them telling bar jokes. *A mother-in-law walks into a bar with a hunk of Swiss cheese tied around her neck.*

He'd been wetting the bed for years. It probably had as much to do with Maureen changing the lock as his infidelity.

He smoked and walked west and thought of a moment, circa '57, fifteen years old, up on Maureen's roof, waiting for her to come up and make out with him. They had come back around to each other, having known each other forever, Connie taken anew by the sight of her at a table with the girls at the previous November's Parish Night. Those were the days. Simple appointments, simple agendas. There you were, kissing so sweet, a summer's afternoon. An ocean liner glided slowly between buildings down the Hudson. In his hand, that first cold beer of the day. The blueness of sky, the raw smell of life up his nose, the slow glide of the ocean liner, the taste of that beer. He worked as a helper for a trucking company called REA Express, so he had a little money. But the thought that stuck, the thought he never shook from that moment up on Maureen's roof: *I cannot picture life without it.* It meaning not love, or sex, or Maureen, or kissing, or a blue sky, or ocean liners, or money, or health—but alcohol. Can't imagine life without it. A drink, a beer, something. Wrapped up tight already, fifteen years old. In his gut, he knew. *Otherwise,* went the premonition, *I just won't make it.*

And who the hell is this David anyway?

Back in his room the bourbon tasted like someone had watered the bottle down. He wondered where the kick had gone, the sting at the back of the throat.

The Starlit Diner as a destination contained an element of surprise Connie did not care for. "Why didn't you let me know, David?" Connie whispered to himself. "What kind of sneak-attack nonsense is that?" He sat in the dark, whispering, smoking, drinking.

He went to the closet, reached up to a shelf, and produced by its handle a tiny portable television. A thirteen-inch screen, the weight of a man's bowling ball. He pushed the hot plate back out of the way, unraveled the TV's cord. After the tubes warmed he sat transfixed by the muted black-and-white images of a *Combat!* re-run. Connie would not have been surprised if a guy like Vic Morrow enjoyed a drink. Again came a respectful knock.

"Yes?" Connie said, going for an official tone.

"You took off abruptly. Are you all right?" David said, popping his head into the room.

"Why would I be anything other than all right?" Connie said. "Come in if you're coming in."

David sat down and said, "You seemed to leave all of a sudden, that's all."

"You knew they were coming."

"Yes."

"Your cronies."

"Cronies?"

"Do you have something you want to say to me?" Connie asked, his voice going thin with vulnerability.

"I have no idea what you're talking about."

"Uh-huh."

"We took a walk together."

"Go on," Connie said, draining his glass and refilling it. "Don't worry, I can drink and listen at the same time."

"I think you're being a little—"

"What? A little what?" Connie pulled on his cigarette, boxed it up, blew the smoke out with ill-defined hostility. "Go ahead, explain it. Was it something about me, personally?"

"I don't know what you want explained."

"Me, at Bickford's this morning with my Hefty bag. What, if a room opens up, you get your mark settled in, that how it works?" His voice didn't slur, but there was something wild in his eyes, his movements subtly possessed.

"My *mark*?"

"You a friend of my wife's?" Connie said.

"I have no idea what you're talking about."

"Why would you, hmm?"

"You're drunk, and somehow got it into your head I set out to shanghai you in some way."

"You said it, not me. Your words," and somewhere in the far reaches of his mind Connie thought, *Poor David, having to put up with my nonsense.* "Did you hear one of your pals, what he said to me?"

"What?"

"Am I a wet one, David? Is that what this is about?"

"Look, I'm sorry if you thought—"

"Live and let live," Connie said. "Isn't that one of your organization's dictums?"

Vic Morrow gave orders in the battlefield to someone on the TV. Connie polished off the contents of his glass, poured another, and said, "Don't you think I've given some thought as to the nature of my drinking, vis-à-vis its ramifications?"

"Really, it's not my—"

"I met your leaders, believe me. Years ago. Sure, Alcoholics Anonymous. Yeah. I know the deal. I sold newspapers to those guys started the whole fucking thing. Early fifties, I was a kid. Used to be a clubhouse right over here on 24th."

"You know about that clubhouse?" David said.

"It's gone: 24th, Ninth and Eighth. They tore the whole block down, but the main guy—"

"Bill?"

"With the big ears. He used to grab the stack of newspapers out of my arms, peel off a five-dollar bill—I'm nine years old."

"You sold them newspapers?"

"He'd throw a football around with me out on the street, Bill. First place I ever saw a television set, front room of that clubhouse. They all wore suits, the men, like a custom of the time. I'd walk out of there with a five-dollar bill and a bottle of Coca-Cola. See, the thing is," Connie said, and poured some more liquor into his glass, "there's a couple type of drinkers. Says so in your Big Book."

"You're familiar with the Big Book?" David said. It was the affectionate name of the main text of Alcoholics Anonymous, officially titled *Alcoholics Anonymous*.

Connie had attended an AA meeting or two on his own visits to Bellevue years ago and was handed some of the literature. "I am. Are you?"

"Yes."

"You should be—you're a member, correct?"

"Correct," David said, glancing around, as if planning his escape.

"I have no personal grudge against the outfit. Besides which, the book says it plain: they draw a line, crystal clear, between what *they* describe as an alcoholic—*they*, follow me—as opposed to what you might call a hard or let's say heavy drinker. And I would say, my case, long as we're talking"—and here Connie broke wind, let one rip, a perverse punctuation mark in service to his speech, which sounded like a cardboard box getting violently ripped open—"would, according to *their* standards, fall somewhere in the category of what might be called a hard or heavy drinker. Granted. You know, speaking generally."

David looked at him a moment before bursting into laughter.

"Don't hurt yourself there, David," Connie said. "Easy does it," he added with a bizarre wink.

After a little while David could not stop yawning, and Connie said, "Go ahead and yawn your way out of here."

He sat alone in the dark, save for the snow on the television screen. He got to his feet and considered this question: how does a nonalcoholic get ready for bed? He decided to brush his teeth. He reserved toothbrushing for the morning as a rule, but given the night's events he thought he'd brush before bed as a demonstration of his nonalcoholic nature. People of an alcoholic nature go to bed without brushing, he figured, and given the fact that he was not an alcoholic, he probably should brush. And then he thought, *What else does a person who's not an alcoholic do?* His mind drew a blank. Then he thought, *I know what I can do, I can prepare my clothes for the morning. I can lay my clothes out so when I wake up I know what I'm going to wear. People of nonalcoholic natures do such things. If I'm not an alcoholic,* he thought, *and I'm not, I can lay my clothes out like a nonalcoholic in preparation for tomorrow's nonalcoholic day. Granted, I like to drink. Vic Morrow probably enjoys a drink himself.* He got up and looked at his clothes in the closet and thought, *What a strange thing to do,* and decided against it. *I'm not going to put my clothes out for tomorrow just to prove I'm not an alcoholic. If I'm not an alcoholic, why do I have to prove it? I don't have to prove my nonalcoholic nature to anybody. And who would I be proving it to anyway? And even if I am an alkie, whose business is that?*

They had tried to help his father, those men in suits. They came up to the house, spoke to his mother, the half-heard conversations lodged in Connie's memory. A strange word when you're seven years old: *anonymous.* Their clean-shaven faces, their pressed suits, a lucidity in the eye. Whispered words between his mother and those men, seeping through fabric hanging from doorway curtain rods, one doorless doorway after the next in those railroad flats, curtain after curtain through which muffled words floated.

Did they know Connie's father killed himself? Of course they knew. They came to the house, tried to help, prior to the move uptown. They knew Sammy. And then, back in Chelsea, after the six-month nightmare that was Harlem, they paid Connie and his siblings special attention. They bought out Connie's stack of newspapers nightly, tipped him heavily, gave him cold bottles of Coca-Cola from the red machine that tasted so good. Those men in suits, that AA clubhouse right there on 24th, they tried, didn't they?

Motherfuckers at that diner, and David playing dumb. Go ahead, David, keep playing dumb, see what happens.

He decided on some light housecleaning like a non-alcoholic might. He picked up the ashtray, escorted it across the room, and was going to dump its contents out the window—but caught himself about to perform the act of an alcoholic. Your first night in the house and you want to dump your ashtray directly over the entranceway?

He laid down and prayed aloud: "Lord God Father, please hear my prayer. Bless Maureen and Artie and Stevie, grant them peace and watch over them, Father." He called his god *Father* because he liked it that way. He never did have too much of an earthly father.

That man for a time up in Harlem, after Sammy and Edward passed, the man who taught Connie how to find the constellations in the sky. From that spot in St. Nicolas Park, surrounded by the night, away from the streetlamps (to let the stars shine more bright, the man said). The man's breath on Connie's neck, crouching behind him, the heaviness of an arm on Connie's shoulder. The smell of talc on the man, a porkpie hat on his head. Did the man show Connie care and concern—was he really about astronomy? Holding Connie in a specific manner by the arms, directing his body to face a certain angle, to line up a constellation in the sky. *The guy had his hands on me quite a bit: like that priest who taught me how to make free throws. They always position themselves behind you, these short eyes. They sure know how to pick out a fa-*

therless kid, let me tell you. Eagle eyes for the fatherless ones. See a kid with no father coming a mile off, a short eyes can. The special talent of any moderately gifted pedophile.

I cannot picture life without it. He tried to feel out in his mind for an image of himself as a person who did not drink, and nothing came. The construct of a character named Connie Sky who lived a sober life eluded him, terrified him down to the ground, made him shudder.

An alcoholic walks into a bar.

He felt his consciousness abandoning itself, the gears of his thoughts slipping, failing to catch altogether, and his last internal ramble came as a refrain, a fervent appeal tinged by the martyrdom of his suffering.

Let me go, Connie's heart cried, *let me go, let me go.*

ARTHUR AND HIS FRIENDS

Nothing was off-limits, especially not the dead. The body still warm and these kids pounced. Sometimes there were ground rules—no mothers, say—but not with these kids. Everything went with these kids.

They met up intuitively, without appointment, in various late-night stairwells, on various floors and buildings of the Chelsea Projects: 466 or 443, 288 or 446, 427 or 426 or 428.

Albert, Errol and Joey, Rennie, Michael, Arthur. The six of them high on reefer usually, but nobody was holding. They were talking about getting their hands on a bottle of Carbona, an automotive cleaning agent you poured into a handkerchief and huffed, but they never got around to it, so they sat there sounding on each other. Twelve, thirteen, fourteen years old, they spat between their legs, making art on the stairwell steps, one o'clock in the morning, talking about each other's families.

Somebody said something hysterical, which caught Rennie by surprise, and snot shot from his nose. A dark-skinned Puerto Rican, the kind they sometimes call *chocolatte*. His father collected welfare and talked on a CB station.

Albert, Puerto Rican, quite physical in his humor: he'd grab you and rub his head into the middle of your

chest like a dog. Later, Albert would go to prison for sell-
ing drugs, and the experience wrung the laughter from
him for good.

Errol and Joey, two brothers, their family something
of a project anomaly in that they were Jews. (Or, at 2
percent of the population, are Jews an anomaly the world
over?)

Michael, black and Puerto Rican, yet fair-skinned and
nerdy. His father had a vaguely effeminate manner about
him.

"Artie," Errol said one night, "I wanted to ask you a
question about your dead grandfather."

Arthur grinned, let the saliva hang as close as he could
get it to the stairwell step, before he sucked it back up.

Maureen's father had gotten an apartment of his own
in 443. She would make a monthly pot of tripe, and Arthur, who hated the smell of it, delivered it at arm's length
across the yard to his grandfather. He and Steven would
watch TV and eat potato chips and drink Pepsi-Cola over
there. Once they watched *Hans Christian Andersen*, starring Danny Kaye, and Arthur felt so safe on the couch
next to his grandfather, who died two years ago at the age
of fifty-three, a subway staircase heart attack.

"That white-haired motherfucker used to walk
around like a ghost, remember?" The kids made sounds
to inspire Errol to find a groove for his riff. "Who told
that son of a bitch to go and die? I wasn't done with him
yet."

Arthur let his spit collapse onto the step. "Oh yeah,
and what about your bald-headed Jew father? That fuck's
probably having anal sex with Michael's father right this
minute."

"Say what?" Michael said.

"Like your father's not a faggot."

"Look who's talking," Rennie said.

"Oh, don't get me started on your fat fucking father," Arthur said to Rennie, "sitting up there in front of his base station, talking to some spic truck drivers, collecting welfare, smoking his L&Ms, that crippled stupid Puerto Rican fuck. Big nasty ashtray on the windowsill, you saw it, Albert—Errol, you seen it, all them empty Rheingolds— talking to who-the-fuck-knows on that stupid base station. It's like your father's our age. He's a fucking grown-up—what the fuck is he doing talking on a base station all day long, can you answer me that? Albert, let me get a cigarette."

"Least I got a father," Rennie said quietly.

Arthur, sensing a trap, responded cautiously. "I got a father."

"You call that drunken-ass bum a father?" Rennie said, and the kids made a sound, feeling Rennie's rhythm. "That white-milk son of a bitch, stumbling around, his stupid-ass doorman's uniform. I bet he sleeps in that shit too. That bastard's never been sober, not a day in his life, long as I been seeing his ass, since we're babies in baby carriages that son of a bitch been drunk. It's amazing when you think about it, a truck hasn't ran his ass over yet. That that motherfucker's still alive is a bigger-ass miracle than the Miracle on 34th Street."

"That right?" Arthur said.

"Out of all the drunk-ass alcoholic fathers in these projects," Rennie said, "and I'm sitting up in this hallway with the son of the one who takes the cake."

"Worse than Kenny's father?" Albert said.

Rennie reflected. "Okay, nah, nobody's as bad as Kenny's father, that's too hard to beat. But Mr. Sky in his stupid-ass doorman's uniform, sleeping on benches and shit? At least my father sleeps in a bed, Artie. I saw your father take a piss in a telephone booth on Ninth the other day, middle of the afternoon, fucking doorman uniform had all kinds of stains on it and shit, old ladies and little kids walking by, tell me I'm lying. Shame on your father, that intoxicated douchebag. Looked like a straight-up crazy-ass drunken bum on the street, which, when you think about it, basically that's what he is." Rennie had found a stride, and the stairwell buzzed. "If I didn't know he was your father, Artie, I would have pushed his ass in the river and watched him drown just to pass the time a good while ago."

"That right?" Arthur said. Rennie's deluge threw him. He tried to consider Rennie's mother but could not call up any details. You needed details, specifics—that's the funny part. "And what about your mother?" Arthur said, but his tone held a lost quality and gained no traction.

Joey said, "I saw Mr. Sky take a shit on his own couch one day—remember that, Artie? Pants down to his ankles, his own living room. Motherfucker thought he was in the Grant's Bar bathroom."

"Amazing when you think about," Rennie said, "he still got a job, 'cause that motherfucker, all he does is drink, did you notice that? That scumbag's always packing a taste. He don't blink without a drink your father, Artie. Son of a bitch'll be drunk at his own funeral, which by the way should be any minute."

Arthur kept his head down, and the kids watched him.

"Let's be real," Rennie said. "Tell me that mother-fucker don't urinate in the bed three times a week and I'll eat my straw hat."

"Oh shit," Albert said.

"Ho snap," Michael said.

"Bitch is crying," Errol said.

It happened sometimes. The point, in fact, to find a soft spot, to hemorrhage somebody.

"See what you did, Rennie?" Albert said.

"Your mother," Arthur said through tears. "Mother's so fat." But his thoughts couldn't find their way. "She's like . . . a blob . . . like I don't know where your mother's titties end . . . and her pussy begins."

"That's dry," Rennie said.

"Like a desert breeze," Michael chimed in.

"Speaking of mothers," Joey said, "I'll tell you the truth, Artie, straight up: I'd like to fuck your mother. Is this possible?" They all laughed, Arthur included, wiping his face. "Square business," Joey said, "you think I could catch a rap with your mother?"

They were, each of them but one, virgins.

"Oh shit! Reminds me of a rumor I heard," Errol said, "that Jondie and Ray-Ray fucked Ritchie Velasco's mother at the same time, you heard that?"

"That's not true," Michael said.

"How you know it's not true? Your faggoty-ass father carries a pocketbook on a strap."

"It's a satchel, moron," Michael said.

"Two on one can be okay," Joey opined, "but I'm not in the mood to share Mrs. Sky: thanks but no thanks." They roared at Joey's delivery. "I want that pussy all to myself, and if that makes me selfish I sincerely apologize.

Artie, I'll be a good stepfather to you and Stevie. Take you to Whelan's counter every Sunday, let you split an egg cream."

Arthur leaned back and howled at the flashing mental image of Joey as his stepfather.

CHAPTER THREE

SUSAN ENTERED CONNIE'S ROOM BRINGING KISSES, and they went on to make love in quiet morning fashion. In the shower Connie genuflected before her and soaped her up good, starting with her feet. He washed her bottom like it was his own bottom, and he scrubbed her back gently with long flowing strokes of the cloth. He took the showerhead and rinsed her thoroughly. Susan reached for the cloth and started to wash him. "No," Connie said, "leave me." She mock-frowned and got out.

He took a guzzle of bourbon to set the pins of his mentality straight. There was a full-length mirror inside the closet door, and as he put on his uniform he wondered if anybody had ever seen him for who he was, wondered if he himself knew who he was. There was a school of philosophy which dismissed identity. *To know oneself: give me a break. You show me somebody claiming to know himself and I'll show you a bullshit artist.* He considered Susan. *I don't know her, but here we are under the same roof and we made good love a few times, so why not leave it alone?* The ability to know somebody—how possible? From day one he had known Maureen. He held his wife's hand during fire drills in first grade. *Have you ever seen me, Maureen? Have I ever seen you?*

On the job he had witnessed poses of identity crumble and dissolve, self's house of cards collapsing despite the finest external trappings—the country homes, the luxury station wagons, the purebred dogs, the wraparound terraces. And at day's end all was mystery, vulnerability, and—life's great equalizer—death. As a doorman he watched the posturing, padded by material wealth, nonetheless fold under the blunt-force trauma of illness, betrayal, and the like. There were tenants who walked by Connie for months, barely acknowledging him, until one day the marriage implodes and the passage through the lobby becomes less cocksure. Life stops you, softens you—an adultery, say, or some serious diagnosis—and there you now sit, openly weeping in the lobby before your doorman, and more than once Connie consoles you with a hug and a few kind words. The job funny that way, offering windows into lives even the closest of family and friends did not access. Women generally liked Connie. Men from old money liked him fine, as well as men who made their money. Younger men living off the wealth of still-living parents he customarily had problems with.

He went to Bickford's, ordered a bacon-and-egg sandwich on a buttered roll to go, took the 1 to Times Square, and caught the shuttle east. He waited at the top of a staircase eating his sandwich, taking the cue of a young black kid waiting with him. They would take whichever came first—the 4, 5, or 6. The kid with his highly attuned ears skipped down the flight and Connie followed.

He entered through the service entrance, a coffee light and sweet from the Greeks in hand.

"Qué pasa, Hector," Connie said.

"Very good, Mr. Con," Hector said, "how is you?"

"You're a good man, Hector, I don't care what they say about you."

"They no saying anything about me," Hector responded, "they saying about you."

"I bet they are." Connie changed into his custodian's uniform. "I'm a utility player, Hector, you know that."

"Yes, Mr. Con."

"I don't fuck around."

"I know you don't."

"Service car, front car, front door, whatever I can do to help this house."

"Me too," Hector said.

"That's why I'm talking to you. We have the same work ethic, a little thing they call character."

"Cartoon character," Hector said.

"How's the front?"

"Quiet."

"Super around?"

"Painting."

"Where?"

"Six," Hector said, "Gillespie."

"Big job?"

"Nah. Small job. Bathroom."

"Thank you, my friend."

"Okay, Mr. Con, you be good."

Connie arranged things to his liking on the service car, got settled with his coffee and a cigarette. With a can of Brasso and a clean strip of old T-shirt, he went to work on the fixtures. "Make it shine, Mr. Con-Con," he said, rocking slightly on a leather stool's tripod of castors. He liked the smell of the chemicals, the pleasing way the brass shined.

The car gave off one short ring from the fifteenth floor. Connie shot up there and swung the door open.

"Game of crib, Con, a little later maybe?"

"Down the office in twenty," Connie said.

"Ten-four," John said.

Everything folded out, the chairs and table, as John went on a run of fives and fifteens in the back stairwell of the ninth floor.

"Look at you," Connie said.

"Look at me," John said sadly, throwing down cards. Lonely as all get-out, what he was. How can six thousand square feet feel claustrophobic?

"How's school?"

"Sucks." He went to an old, established school across the park where he had to wear a blazer. "Did you like school?"

"Me?" Connie said. "I hated school. The nuns and priests, they paddled you on principle."

"I'd like to quit," John said, "but my mother would have a shit-fit."

"Biggest mistake of my life," Connie said, but he didn't mean it.

After a moment John broached a subject with tentative concern: "Something happened."

"What happened?"

"My mother."

"I saw her taking off for Washington."

"This morning. Before she left."

"Okay," Connie said.

"All right," John said. "So I'm just . . . you know. I'm waking up. I get up, I go to take a leak. I go into the kitchen. You know, like, still half asleep."

"I got you."

"And so . . ." John said, looking inwardly, recalling it, reliving it, "so I go to make a bowl of cereal. Like I always do."

"Rice Krispies?"

"Special K."

"Continue."

John chuckled nervously. "So I'm making the cereal. And my mother. She comes into the kitchen. She's ready to leave for the airport. I'm at the counter, over by the sink. I put some cereal in the bowl. I get the milk out, and I'm about to, you know . . ."

"Pour some milk over the cereal."

"Yeah. And my mother comes over. She comes over. Says something about me needing a haircut. Something like that," John said, trying to recall the beats of the story in their proper order. "And then I think she says, *I'll have Andrea*"—the governess—"*make you an appointment at the salon*. And just then Andrea comes in. And my mother, I don't know, she comes over, and—she puts her hand on my shoulder. And then . . . and then . . . she, like, brushes the hair away from my face."

"Okay," Connie said.

"And then—*boom!*" John reenacted the sudden move and Connie jumped back a bit in his chair.

"Whoa."

"And I tell her, *Don't fucking touch me!*" John shot a quick, worried look at Connie. "I don't curse like that at my mother, Con."

"I know that."

"I say, *Don't fucking touch me.* I smack her hand away and slam the milk down on the counter, like a half gallon.

I had just opened it and it explodes, and I push my mother across the room. She almost falls, but Andrea catches her! The milk's all over the place—the whole kitchen's white! In Andrea's hair. My mother had to change her clothes." John stopped a moment to consider Connie, who offered no hint of an opinion one way or another.

"Then what?"

"I don't know. I say, *Don't fucking touch me*, and I slam the milk down—and she goes stumbling back into Andrea—and I say, *You have one daughter, not two!*" John stopped again to gauge his listener's reaction. "And then I go, *I'll get a fucking haircut when I feel like it—I'll go to a fucking barber, not your goddamn* salon."

After a moment Connie said, "And what'd your mother do?"

"Just—she looked shocked. We were all shocked. She said *Well* a few times. Just, *Well*. And then she looks at her wrist, where I smacked it. She says we'll talk about it when she returns. She goes to change. Andrea starts to clean up, I tell her get out, and I clean up."

After a long moment Connie said, "You didn't do anything wrong, if that's what you're worried about. Things like this, they happen, you know, in families." He picked up his pack of Camels off the table and shook one out.

"Can I get one, Con?"

He'd given John cigarettes before but felt bad about it. With a small frown he gave the pack a second shake and John snatched one.

Connie lit their cigarettes. John coughed a little, almost choked, and Connie smiled, produced his pint, and took a hit. John extended his hand.

"What?" Connie said.

"Come on, let me wet my whistle."

The stairwell dead quiet, their voices slapping off the walls with a sting. Connie handed him the pint and John took a hit, his face freezing from the shock of booze. He took a drag off his Camel, attempted a few smoke rings.

"Watch," Connie said, demonstrating perfect rings, and performed a French inhale.

"Cool."

"All right, let's play some cribbage," Connie said, "and I apologize in advance."

"Dream on," John said, and he produced a massive joint, picked up Connie's Zippo, striking the flint against his leg. He lit the joint, careful not to set his locks on fire.

"That's one big son-of-a-bitching jaybird."

John passed it to Connie, and he smoked it up, and handed it back to John. Connie took another hit off the pint and handed it to John.

"Whew," Connie said, and John started to laugh. Connie picked up the cards and went to shuffle them and they shot out of his hands onto the floor for a fifty-two-pickup, and they laughed their asses off like you do when you're high.

Connie on his knees started to gather the cards. John lit another joint.

Connie climbed back into his chair, shuffled the cards slowly, no fancy stuff. He looked like he had a concussion. "Wait," he said, looking around on the ground, "are there . . . ? I better count them."

John watched him count the cards. Connie was drooling, spit collecting at his mouth, and John passed him the joint.

Connie toked on it and said, "Okay, now wait a minute." He stared down at the cribbage board.

"What?" John said.

"Forgot how to play," Connie said. John started to laugh hysterically, when Connie raised a sudden hand. "Hold up, hold up."

They both made a show of being quiet. Connie cocked an ear toward the service car.

"Did—"

"Huh?"

Connie listened intensely, shook his head, relit the joint, passed it back to John. "Reefer's got me hearing things. All right, let's play some cribbage."

"Remember how to play?" John said.

They laughed and played.

Then: "Fuck," John said.

"What happened?"

"Ah. Bit my tongue."

"Okay?"

John showed a mix of laughter and pain. "Fucking braces," he said. "Tired of them. Can't eat, can't do shit." Then, on impulse, "I want them out," and he reached into his mouth.

"Don't," Connie said, smacking his hand away.

"Hate them," John said, and then, above them in the stairwell, the sound of a door creaking open.

Footsteps descended the staircase. Connie reached quick for the joint roaches, ate them, and pocketed the pint.

Like the ghost of an old-time journeyman painter, there on the halfway landing of the stairs, dressed in painter's overalls, cigar in hand, stood Walter. They looked at each other a moment in silence.

"Hey, Mr. Mezzola," John chuckled.

"Hi, Walter!" Connie said, too loud.

Walter looked down at them, eyes tight with confusion, Connie and John seated across from each other at the small table, cribbage board before them.

John stared down at the table and started to crack up. The more he attempted not to laugh, the redder his face got, his body convulsing in fits.

"He all right?" Walter said.

"No, you know what it is, Walter . . . he . . . recently, just got braces," Connie said.

"Yeah?" Walter said, as John held his face in his hands, sobbing, his whole body shaking.

"Ahhhhh!" John cried.

"Go ahead," Connie said, "let it out."

"Ahhhhhh!"

"They put the damn things in wrong," Connie said.

"For the teeth," Walter said.

"Yeah, yeah, so he's in pain, and so he doesn't know what to do with himself. He gets a little . . . I don't know."

Walter stayed quiet for a moment. He had to be careful. Everybody tippy-toed around the kid's family. The kid's mother could have Walter packing by the weekend. She wasn't on the board but the board kissed her ass, recognizing the value of her tenancy. With John's mother in the house you sit back and watch the price of your apartment go up. "Do me a favor," he said to Connie. "My office."

"Be right there, Walter."

The super turned and went back up the staircase. They heard the door creak open and shut.

"You in trouble?" John said.

"Nah, nah," Connie said, "it'll be okay."

"Because if you want . . ." John said, laughing and crying.

"Nah, don't worry," Connie said. He looked at the battleship gray on the walls, and imagined himself sitting inside the upended, gutted carcass of an elephant.

John produced a small vial of Visine.

"Let me get some."

John handed the vial to Connie. He tilted his head back and tried not to blink, but the drops missed his eyes and rolled down his face like tears.

"Probation as it is," Walter said, holding more fire to his cigar. "Playing games in the hall with the kid like that. How you figure such a thing's all right?"

Connie thought he could see Walter attempting to sound like the superintendent of the house, which he was, but why do you have to try to sound like it?

"Listen to me careful, now, what I'm going to say," Walter began. Connie watched him build a head of steam consistent with a boss who's ready to chastise a worker, when Walter's wife appeared in the room.

"Hey, Miss Mezzola," Connie said.

She nodded at him, a woman of few words. "Ready?"

"Yeah," Walter said.

"Here?" she said.

"Why not," he said, and she popped away.

"Still busting my chops, Saxton. By the way, forget the game-playing in the hall."

"Does she know I'm represented by a labor union?"

"Look, Con, you know, I know: they want you gone, you go."

"Not why I pay dues."

"Got to write you up again."

"Write me up?"

"Insisting."

"That hurts me."

"Hurts me too," Walter said. "What's wrong with your eyes?"

"What?"

"Bloodshot, here to Jersey."

Connie lit a cigarette.

"I don't know what to do," Walter said. His hands were spotted with tiny specks of paint, the rims of his nails pleasingly caked with plaster. "Trying to help you get on track, which case I don't have to terminate you."

His wife appeared with two plates of baked ziti, some salad and bread on the side. From the front pockets of her housecoat she produced two bottles of Coca-Cola. She opened them with a bottle opener, dropped a fork on each plate, and disappeared.

"Oh my God," Connie said.

"Go ahead," Walter said.

Connie dug in, hungry from the reefer.

"Son of a."

"Hot, watch."

Connie drank some Coke. "Delicious," he said.

"So maybe," Walter said, "if you talk to Saxton."

"Talk to her."

"*Miss Saxton, I'm sorry I got fresh with a friend of yours,* simple, like that."

"Me, got fresh?"

"*Please forgive me, and in the meantime I'll watch my Ps and Qs, and I hope you can forgive me, Miss Saxton,* some shit like that."

"This ziti's incredible."

"Like a second thought for my wife, that ziti, a third thought. Because otherwise they insist on something in the file come the time for me to terminate you. I mean, look, Con, you cannot skate on your buff job forever."

"Got friends in this house. Saxton ain't shit."

"On the board she is."

"I got people on this board," Connie said, his mouth full, his face down close to the plate on Walter's desk, "way before Saxton ever thought about coming here."

"And these days sometimes they don't even let you collect in the meantime."

"Hah?"

"Last guy I got out. Charles. Remember Charles?"

"Yeah?"

"Management fought him on the unemployment. To let you know I say this. 'Cause the thing is, if you back down with her just a little, Saxton, swallow your pride two seconds, because I would hate to see you go."

"Thank you, Walter."

"Go ahead. Eat."

Walter picked up his fork and did some eating himself, and he said, "Let me ask."

"Yeah."

"The kid."

"John."

"He all right?"

"What sense?"

"You play games with him in the hall."

"Once in a while. If I got a little time."

"What do you talk about?" Walter asked.

"Whatever," Connie said. "You know, he's a kid."

"My point."

"Thing of it is," Connie said, "he's lonely."

"That right?"

"I don't know . . . I'm like a father figure in a way."

They ate a little bit, and now it was Walter's turn to laugh.

"What?" Connie said.

"Nah, it's just . . . it's funny is all! You, a father figure to him! I don't know why," Walter said, and you would think he had been smoking some strong reefer of his own. "I could see you showing up to the family compound they got up there, yeah, yeah, and you show up in your doorman's uniform!"

"That's funny."

"Yeah, yeah, and you say, *I'm John's new father!*" Through laughter he added, "And, and who knows, maybe you end up marrying the mother!"

They laughed some more about Connie becoming the newest member of the famous political clan, before Walter got up, grabbed the plates off his desk, and left Connie alone.

He went downstairs, took a dreamless nap on his bed of cement, got up, and got busy. He did a garbage run, bagged it up nice, and left it just inside the service entrance. He checked with the guys working the front to see if they needed anything. He delivered some dry cleaning and a few packages. The mail came and Connie cased it, throwing letters into slots with accuracy and speed. He rolled the cart onto the service car and delivered the mail upstairs. He prepped the bucket in the slop-sink room and mopped the back stairwell landings, a salty bead of sweat stinging one eye. He hosed off the service en-tranceway, swept the area of leaves and other detritus, and when he was done with that he grabbed the can of Brasso and some rags and headed toward the front of the house, where he spotted Larry outside.

Larry as a rule had two cameras hanging on him, and attached to the straps, like beads on a necklace, a string of 35mm film canisters. He had bad skin, rough and uneven—*like his personality*, Connie thought. You could read the whole shitty history of Larry's life by the map of pockmarks on his face.

"There he is, Mr. Fucko in a dirty-ass pickup," Connie said. Larry sat in the passenger seat of his Datsun, a black California license plate hammered with yellow glyphs.

"See this one here," Larry said, displaying a camera.

Connie held up the can of Brasso and, as if a courte-ous afterthought, said, "Would the supercilious parasite like a taste?"

"This one has no film in it," Larry said. "I carry it with fuckers just like you in mind."

"You try it."

"Keep rattling my cage," Larry said with scary Cali-fornia slowness, "I just might."

Connie turned the corner onto Fifth. He polished the standpipe off the house's front entrance. As it started its descent over the park, the sun gave a direct hit, and the brass responded with a glisten. He sauntered over to the canopy poles and saw Ramey and Slovell in the Impala across the street, an early-season ball game wafting from the vehicle.

George appeared. An older man from Ireland, George had worked the house a very long time.

"How are you, George?"

George, Connie suspected, resented having to share the tenants with the rest of the staff, such was the greedy nature of the man's obsequiousness. Connie tried to befriend him any number of times but finally gave up, dismissing him as a sycophant. In more generous moments Connie considered another take: George had seen one too many coworkers come and go, and it hurt too much to bond with a man only to have him depart. This take, more forgiving, exposed the soft underbelly of George's standoffish posture, and Connie tried to choose it.

He made the poles of the canopy shine. How had things gotten so contentious with Larry? How had it come to that?

"Am I good or what, Mr. George?"

"You missed a spot there," George said. He gave Connie a vicious smile.

"Go play in traffic, George."

The afternoon sun warmed Connie's back. He worked on his knees, rubbing the Brasso into the pole with a strip of T-shirt, as his mind went soft with a sadness. The sun setting over the park, and the listless vehicles moving down Fifth, and how is it that any of these buildings ever got built in the first place? Things could stop adding up, and the world's steady, inconsiderate pulse would not hesitate to shoot a shiver of despair into him.

The harsh exchange with Larry. The agents across the street. The assignment had a crappy reputation, and not one of them seemed to care for it. Last year one agent, trying to keep up on foot with the kids in a Midtown crowd, drew his sidearm in wits-end frustration, letting off a round over the roof of a taxicab which nearly ran him over. The incident made the papers and the agent got reassigned.

The housephone buzzed, George went inside. Connie worked until both poles shone brilliant in the sun. He thought of a song he liked and smiled, thought of his children and Maureen, of Susan and David and Justin in the rooming house.

Connie had been taught the principles of Christianity. Religion didn't sustain, and his churchgoing faded at puberty, though he enjoyed for a time his service as an altar boy and the theatrical qualities associated with the altar/ stage, the sacristy analogous to what he heard Johnny Carson refer to as the greenroom, where players waited to be called onto the show.

His mind's ability to produce intense hatred for people, places, inanimate objects. He feared he did not know how to love, to show love, to receive love—his darkest fear.

Larry, for money, took pictures of people who did not want their pictures taken. He lived to be hated, got his rocks off playing the antagonist, yet Connie also sensed a vulnerability at the core of Larry's mortal soul.

He read something in a book as regards any person you wanted to hit over the head with a hammer, that beyond rehearsing how you would strike the blow, to help release the violent impulse you might instead imagine them as a child.

Before they became enemies, Connie didn't know Larry as a paparazzo staking out the house for photos of the president's widow and her kids. Larry, without a camera in sight, said hello a few times, and they sat on the wooden bench against the stone wall of the park together, conversing easily. Larry, Connie thought, had problems, but wasn't a pathological liar. Connie did not believe Larry fabricated a history from whole cloth to deceive him. No, Larry spoke from a genuine place to serve a specific deception. Larry wasn't afraid to make comments like *I don't know* or *I'm not sure*. Dyed-in-the-wool bullshit artists have an answer for everything.

Larry bonded with Connie to get inside information about the family's itineraries. He used real-life circumstances to betray Connie, the connection founded on a fallacy.

"Good enough," Walter said, out of his painter overalls. He turned to head up Fifth.

"Your brother?"

"Yeah." Walter's brother worked as a super in a house on 98th.

Connie got up and examined the poles from a variety of angles. *You polish over here, it shines over there*, someone once said. *A sacred power bears holy witness to every effort we make.* He lit a smoke and walked across the street, the temperature seven degrees cooler beneath the shade of the park. He hopped up to the top slat of the bench where he used to hang with Larry, prior to their friendship's reversal.

Ramey and Slovell looked at Connie, their moving mouths on display through the windshield. Connie assumed himself their subject, given how they stared. Let them talk. Beads of sweat evaporated on Connie's back from his brass-cleaning efforts, as he inhaled the verdant scent of nature behind him in the park.

A man across the street turned into the house. After a moment George appeared at the sidewalk's edge and pointed Connie out. The man went to the corner and waited for the light to change. A bit of confusion in his step, which Connie thought a pose. Pseudoconfusion. Connie watched the man approach.

"How you doing?" Connie said, jutting his face at him.

"Not bad," the man said, "and yourself?"

"So far so good."

"Okay, so," and the man double-checked the manila envelope he carried, "are you, let's see, Cornelius Sky?"

"Yes."

"Okay," the man said, and handed it to Connie. "I wish I could say it was good news."

"What is it?" Connie felt its weight, his hand a scale, the nine-by-twelve envelope a dark gift, and they were playing a guessing game.

"An order of restraint."

"Order?"

"But it's really not my place," the process server said.

"No, please."

"From your wife. You're separated or something, right?"

"Okay—I mean, yes."

"The order makes reference to your habit of showing up in the middle of the night."

"Does the order use the word *habit*?"

"Good question," the man said. "It states it wasn't a one-shot deal, that it was a recurring incident, and believe me, I'm not judging. It's nice around here."

Connie straightened out the fasteners and removed a sheaf of stapled pages. He couldn't read for his racing mind, only picked up words here and there. He went through the motions one goes through when shocked.

His eyes scanned Maureen's name, his name, a legalistic maxim here and there.

"I wouldn't take it too personal," the man said. "It's a form, basically, and they type in different—"

Connie hopped off the bench and left the man mid-sentence before he spun and said, "Your shtick is tired—stop playing dumb, you little bullshit artist," then trotted across the avenue. He grabbed the Brasso and rags, moved past the Datsun showing no sign of Larry through the service entrance.

On the cement bags he perused the order: *Showing up in a state of severe drunkenness at various late-night hours, on numerous occasions . . . Attempting to enter the apartment using violent means, beating his fists against the door and yelling obscenities . . . Attempting to break into the premises . . . thereby frightening both the children and Mrs. Sky.*

The basement collected a late-afternoon dampness and he caught a chill. He liked the smell of the bags, smelling of a concrete thing. He put the sheaf of pages back into the envelope and let it rest on his chest. The housing cops probably put her up to it. He folded his arms behind his head, closed his eyes. A space opened up behind his breastplate, the spot in his body where he believed tears originated. It hurt so good to be served an order of restraint. *I'm such a terrible creature, a ghoul of the first order. What has become of me? An order of restraint? Violence is not my thing. Beyond which, to put a hand on a woman? A child? Order of restraint, are you kidding me? Who ever the fuck protected me?*

He curled tight onto his right side. His mind had its way with him a while, when he heard a noise: the zipper on a solitary pair of jeans banging against the spinning metal drum of a dryer. Which reminded him. He got up, went and removed the lint from the machines, cleaning each mesh basket with one sweep of his hand, removing the lint all in one piece if he could, as it brought him a pleasure to do so. He put the garbage out on the sidewalk before calling it a day at the job.

He made a few stops on his way downtown and arrived at the rooming house feeling no pain. There wasn't much in this world—not a birth, not a death, not an order of restraint—which a drink could not help to facilitate.

He let himself into his room and noticed a stain on the window shade, and with it came a small wave of pity. "Go ahead then," he whispered to his emotion, "do what you're going to do." He sniffed the air and walked across the hall.

"You're just in time," Susan said. "Are you hungry?"

And Connie knew in her smile, seeing her face, and a glance at the food on the hot plate, that their connection was a lost cause. Or that he himself was the lost cause. They might see each other awhile longer, this might be the end of it, who knew? The sex connection was strong but a partnership was not in the cards, and it produced a sad recognition as he stood in her doorway. Anger flash-flooded his system regarding this life—and why do we know we're going to die, could someone explain it to him?

"I could eat," he said.

"Come in, why don't you?"

She wrapped her arms around him and they kissed once, twice. The simmering concoction featured carrots and potatoes and meat, sweet and pungent.

She wore a skirt and a T-shirt displaying the portrait of a good-looking black woman with a perfectly shaped Afro.

Susan had attended Goddard College in the 1960s, one of those progressive, liberal outposts up in the Green Mountains of Vermont, more therapeutic community than institute of higher learning. The events of her life since graduating, as she would later share with Connie, included a stint of midlevel drug dealing. She and her husband moved cocaine by the kilo, Susan herself the Colombian mule. She had until last summer hung with the SDS crowd, the Weathermen, people like that, before everything fell apart and she managed to wash up in this rooming house, if not well, at least alive and not in prison.

"Do you like Indian food?" She liked to cook and bake, a pleasure inherited from her Oklahoma mother. She produced a canister, tapped out some spices into the simmering food, and gave it a stir.

"Would you mind taking that shirt off?" Connie said.

"Right this minute?"

Some writing under the portrait of the woman: *Free Assata!* and below it, *Break the Chains!*

"Could you put another shirt on? I like how it fits you, but I don't like her."

"Who?"

"*Her*," Connie said. "Joanne Chesimard. I don't care for her. I don't dig her. I don't dig what she's about."

Susan looked at him a moment, cleared her throat. "Why?"

"Why? A stone killer's why. The trooper she and her friends gunned down, and here ten minutes later she rates as a fucking folk hero on a T-shirt? Are you *joking*?"

Susan waited a moment before she spoke. "Do you want to talk about killers? Do you?"

They managed, mainly through strategic silences placed into the conversation by Susan, which served as speed bumps to Connie's drunken self-righteousness, to navigate away from a blowout. But she did not remove the shirt.

One morning at his 34th Street Blarney Stone, Connie read a quote in the *New York Times* by a self-styled revolutionary: *You identify the enemy by the uniforms they wear.* A picture of the guy, goatee and beret, posing on the steps of Columbia's library. It sounded like such idiotic dogma and infuriated him. Civil-service jobs were held up as something of a boon where Connie came from, to get work as a cop or garbageman or fireman, and these jobs required, well, a uniform. He knew the guy in the paper was speaking in metaphor, but still. And here you got a dead trooper on the Taconic over a routine broken taillight stop who was making, what, fourteen an hour plus all the overtime he can grab to keep the kids in parochial school?

And it wasn't just the likes of Joanne Chesimard who stirred Connie's ire, because he could in fact imagine the thousand daily indignities, intended or not, thrown at black people from, yes, the pigs—but not just the pigs, all white people practically. But none of it justified murder. *Call it hateful retribution, call it spiteful payback, and I'll hear you, but don't tell me you identify the enemy by the uniforms they wear, don't say that stupid shit to me.*

What really burned Connie's ass was these rich white kids. Embarrassed by their family money, their trust funds, and Greenwich Village town houses, they set about to apologize for their good fortune, the power of their shame sufficient to fuel the building of bombs. Go ahead and blow it all up, take the whole fucking block with you, why don't you?

They talked this stuff over, Connie in his doorman's uniform, drinking liquor and eating Indian food on Susan's narrow bed. *Why*, Connie thought, *did I bring the whole stupid subject up? Why am I so willfully belligerent? Do I actually give a shit one way or the other? I felt the weight of my fleeting connection to her so I picked a fight. What have I ever committed to? Have I ever stepped up to the plate on behalf of something other than the next drink? That's the question behind my indignation. You envy Joanne Chesimard her courage, robbing banks for something vastly beyond personal avarice. What do I stand for? Anything, anything at all?*

They ate and talked. Susan had a small library. Her "core concentration" was in English (Goddard didn't use traditional words like "major"), and her book stash contained novels, classics mostly, with some good junk thrown in too. *Not a pretentious bone in the woman's body, and here she is feeding me in our shared rooming house, so why would I accuse her of guilt politics?*

They decided to take a walk. Coming out, Susan pointed to a brownstone across the street.

"I used to live there. Me and my husband. We had the ground-floor apartment. Two fireplaces. A private garden in the back. We used to wonder about the lost souls who lived across the street in the rooming house."

A mugginess in the air, the lights of skyscrapers reflecting off low cloud cover, moving up Eighth Avenue.

"What time is it? Maybe we can second-act a show if you want," Connie said.

"Sounds good."

Their pace took on the assurance of destination. They made their way arm in arm past the hysteria of 42nd Street. They looked up 45th, saw a crowd huddled beneath the Morosco's marquee, and turned into the block.

"I don't like violence of any kind," Connie said, apropos of nothing, although Susan understood it referred back to their conversation in her room. "It scares me."

A couple dressed in flowing scarves and shawls moved past them, the man saying, "And the dialogue's so clunky," the woman saying, "Noel Coward he's not."

Connie and Susan cozied up to the intermission crowd, the sidewalk extra bright and warm. Connie looked up into the hundreds of bulbs of the Morosco's canopy, and the images of his dead parents from the dream returned to him, infusing him with sorrow.

Susan told him a story which he accepted as an olive branch. Abbie Hoffman had befriended the Beatles. Abbie, in Lennon's limo, gave John a tour of black Harlem's ghetto as part of a pitch to shake John for some cash for The Cause, the tour evidence as to how fucked The System was. Lennon went home and wrote not a check but some lyrics: *If you want money for people with minds that hate, all I can tell you is brother you have to wait.*

Susan further conceded that the money from her drug-dealing days went nowhere but into her pocket, or up her own nose.

Connie for his part confessed an uncanny knack for having managed to avoid one difficult stand, ever—a life lived loyal to the throughline of his cowardice.

"Selfish in plain English," he said.

"Don't say that," she said, kissing his cheek.

A loud bell sounded intermission's end. Bolstered by a tight mass of bodies, they took tiny, choppy steps into the theater and found two empties down close on the aisle. They held hands and admired the room's grandeur, the chandeliers, the red velvet seats. They swallowed quick hits off Connie's pint before a human hush rose and moved through the room like a wave, as the house lights started to fade.

CHAPTER FOUR

HE CAME TO IN THE ROOMING HOUSE, a noontime sun attempting to sneak its way past the melancholic window shade. Dried blood inside his mouth produced a struggle for air, blood caked to his gums made it hurt to swallow. He went to shift his body on the bed and realized he was dressed, shoes and all. And also he realized he had at least to some extent shat himself.

Accompanying his terrible physical and psychic hangovers were images that evoked a series of shameful winces. Whole sections of drunks rushed back that would make him want to go into hiding—or have a fast drink.

The night before, Connie and Susan had exited the theater together, after catching the second half of Eugene O'Neill's *A Moon for the Misbegotten*, with Jason Robards and Colleen Dewhurst. Smitten by the vision of Miss Dewhurst, Connie recalled strange identification with the character played by Mr. Robards, who seemed hell-bent on self-destruction in an oddly maudlin fashion. He recalled the brightness of the stage when the curtain rose, and how the actors listened to one another, the power of their silences holding the house ever so still.

They went around the corner to McHale's on Eighth

for a few drinks and Susan abruptly took sick. They caught a cab back to the rooming house, where Connie stood over her in the shared bathroom as she threw up, rubbing her back.

He smoked and drank in his room, watching Don Rickles work the audience of *The Tonight Show*. Rickles pulled an elegant, well-spoken Jamaican lady out of her seat, and after setting her up with a few beats of gentility, his arm around her waist, Rickles inquired if the woman would like to come home with him and be his live-in maid.

And there's Johnny, convulsing, swirling behind his desk, choking on a smoke.

Hold on. Everybody laughed at Rickles. Connie didn't watch Carson alone: he stood at the bar in Grant's and watched it on the Motorola.

He ran out of booze. Encountered David on the staircase, accused him of blocking the way, made ridiculous threats.

He lay in bed now, blinking at a fault line in the ceiling's paint job, the heat of shame pressing into his face.

An object poked his back. Connie reached behind himself, produced the rolled-up manila envelope. Some items you hope to misplace, some you can't shake. If the night didn't coalesce with the order of restraint in hand, the blood inside his mouth and nose got explained, and the hangover's fallout intensified.

The distance, Connie thought as he stood at the bar. *You can* spit *from Grant's to my living room. My wife, my kids, my home!*

Whitey asked him who he was talking to, the men looked at him, standing at the end of the bar alone, and chuckled.

Connie stared at his room's bare bulb, ears red with humiliation. He struggled to sit up.

At Grant's he had produced the manila envelope. Took it out, made a show of studying its pages on the bar.

He pushed off the bed, took a few hobble-steps with a semiswollen ankle, apparently, and a semiload in his pants, to the piece of mirror above the room's midget sink. Experience taught him it was never as bad as it looked, and he kept in mind the marvels of a shower and shave. Blood clotted his face here and there, but all was mostly intact.

He had stood outside the bar. He lit a smoke and knew he should make a left, back to the rooming house, just leave it alone, but also knew it wasn't going to happen, the check of his inebriated brainstorm had already cleared. He got it in his head to go see her and that was that. An order of restraint delivered at the job. When did she decide on such a move? He crossed 25th toward 466, deciding to knock, just knock.

He got in the elevator and through the scrim of intoxication practiced a sensible posture, wanting his body to communicate ease and comfort. *Let's reason this situation out, let's come to terms.*

Connie went to the door. He knocked and waited, no big deal. He waited. And then he thought, *Maybe I didn't knock loud enough.* He stood there another moment, and then he thought, *I'll use the whatchamacallit, the knocker. Knock, knock,* Connie went with the knocker, then *knock knock knock,* and waited. He waited with what seemed to him substantial patience.

"Who is it?"

"It's Con, Maureen, I—"

"No," Maureen said. "Didn't you get the thing?"

"I got the—"

"Just go away, Con, please. Believe me, enough now."

Connie waited a moment. "Maureen? Maureen." He stared off, then used the knocker again. And again.

He started with the flat of his hand against the door, four times hard. He waited a moment, and now came the pounding, simply to get to the bottom of this nonsense once and for all, when the door shot open.

"Wasn't locked, knucklehead, could have walked right in."

The sight of the man struck Connie dumb, and he wondered, despite having just heard, he was pretty sure, his wife's voice, if he had wandered off to the wrong apartment, floor, or building. The man wore a T-shirt and dungarees and sneakers.

"What's it going to take?"

"Who?" Connie said.

"She doesn't want to see you, doesn't want to talk to you. That's what the restraint order's about."

"Fuck you doing in my house?"

From inside Maureen called, "Raymond, don't, just leave it alone when he's like this."

"Like what, Maureen? Let this *pig* in my house."

Raymond Pacheco, the housing cop, placed his hand to Connie's chest and shoved him away from the door.

"Fuck off me, piece of shit."

And they started to have a strange fight. Whereas Connie's frame would be categorized by insurance companies as small to medium, Pacheco's was extralarge, and he spent time with the barbells at the Y. He pushed Connie away from the door. Connie flung himself back toward Pacheco, saying, "My wife, my home, my kids." Pacheco deflected Connie's sloppy swings with simple moves learned at the academy.

"You don't listen, do you?" And he started to man-handle Connie, putting him in a full nelson and marching him toward the elevator as if they wore the same pair of pants.

"This how you do your job, fucking pig?" Connie said. "Go around banging all the project women?"

Pacheco yanked open the outer door and shoved Connie inside. When the elevator started down Pacheco took the opportunity to give Connie a few short socks in the mug, then grabbed him by the throat. He let the back of Connie's head slam into the wall of the elevator. And now, as Connie relived it, standing before his mirror: Pacheco held him by the throat with one hand and with the other slapped Connie's face, hard and deliberate. The outlines of Pacheco's imprinted hand-grip at Connie's throat still visible in the reflection. And the slap ended all struggle. Not the pain of it, which to a sober person would have been severe enough, but the shaming facet. Connie stared at Pacheco and fell silent. The elevator arrived on the first floor. They both stood there, silent tears at Connie's eyes.

"Wait," Pacheco said. "Come on. I'm sorry. I'm sorry," he said, and Pacheco hugged Connie awkwardly. He had done something he didn't mean to do.

Connie cried silent tears down his face, bowed his head. The slap seemingly continued to resound off the candy-apple walls of the elevator. Pacheco himself almost cried, slapping a drunk man who, wrong and nasty with the mouth as he might be, still had a case: Maureen his wife, the kids his kids.

Pacheco went back upstairs briefly, came down, and saw Connie sitting on a bench in the yard. "You all right?" he said.

Connie stared off, his face blood-marked, one eye swelling up a bit.

"Can I give you a lift somewhere?" the cop said. Connie stayed quiet. "It doesn't look too bad, just a mouse."

"Slapped me, what you did," Connie said.

"I'm sorry," Pacheco said. "Seriously. I apologize."

Connie took a breath, shot a glance at him. Pacheco turned and walked away, his movements cloaked heavy by remorse. Connie watched him get into a powder-blue Dodge Dart on 26th. Connie watched the cop bump and grind his way out of the tight space, giving the wheel full spins. It looked a little silly, a big man like Pacheco in a small Dodge Dart, and something about the sight already contained a sliver of forgiveness.

He showered and shaved and went to see Manny on Ninth. Connie sat in the back, engulfed by the clicks and hisses of dry-cleaning machinery. Through clothes draped in plastic he spied a customer waiting to be served, a ring on the man's entitled hand smacking the front counter with metronomic impatience. Manny, from the neighborhood, zapped Connie's uniform and shirt, tossed the cap into a stainless steel box, and flipped a switch, zapping it as well. Perched half-naked on a stool, Connie checked his schedule. Friday: a three-to-eleven on the front car.

Manny mentioned a hockey game of Arthur's in Chelsea Park the following morning and encouraged Connie to attend. Connie thanked him, tried to give him money, but Manny refused and Connie left the way he came, out the back, onto the alley adjacent to the Greek church.

He stopped into his 34th Street Blarney Stone. He had befriended the Irish barman, Shane, who had more than once unlocked an early-morning door for Connie.

A lunchtime crowd of white- and blue-collar workers and others less fortunate drank and ate boilerplate from the steam table. Connie sat by the window perusing the paper. Nixon was on his way out. In South Los Angeles the FBI had torched a house to the ground in search of Patty Hearst. The US Army finally admitted causing the torrential rains in the skies over Vietnam through a process called cloud seeding. The view out the window looked like a Ben Shahn painting. Across the street a group of people gathered in a line that curled around on itself like a question mark, before a boxy green crosstown bus swooped down curbside and carried them all east, question answered.

A homeless woman rolled slowly by the Blarney Stone. She parallel parked her shopping cart carefully against the large plate of glass. She entered and slowly approached Connie at his table. She stood over him not saying a word. She wore a plastic trash bag as if made of the finest cashmere. Her short hair looked like a disturbed barber had taken a butter knife to it. There was something regal in her bearing. She wouldn't look at Connie—to do so would be common, improper. She looked off and away, toward the sun, the better for Connie to admire her profile. Her posture spoke of royal lineage, and it appeared as if she had been so kind as to enter this establishment if only to allow Connie a moment's appreciation of her beauty.

Connie picked up the change on the table before

him, thirty-five cents. The woman extended her hand in a manner that said, *Yes, I bequeath you permission to make an offering, if it will help you to do so*, before she slowly turned to exit. Connie watched her pull her cart westward, out of sight.

A little later he found himself walking east on 34th, the still air of spring leaving him vulnerable and weepy, without a witness.

The six months in Harlem had included the spring. The woman with the red bandanna cupped Connie's nine-year-old face in her hands and told him how she loved the springtime, as she worked a small plot of dirt in front of her building across the way.

His father had turned the oven on. Edward taken by accident became the story. Thought himself alone in the house, Sammy did. Edward, asleep on a bed in the back, hands folded in silent repose, ready-made for his child coffin.

His father pulled a suicide, how people spoke of it, as if to say his father had pulled a fast one, suicide a thing you got away with, a number you pull.

505 West 132nd, two flights up facing the back, and there in the bedroom with his mother now, Pete Cullen. They had apparently married. He wore green work pants and boots. A troubled man, Cullen, and no answer would ever arrive as to why Connie's mother married him, or why he married her, a woman with (now only) four young children.

Connie one day sidled up and asked if he could call him Dad. Pete Cullen said, "I'll put your fucking head through that wall." Pointing with terrible violence, punctuating his words with a forefinger.

Of all the kids, he got beat most, Connie did, whipped

and slapped, pushed and shoved and lifted straight up by
the hair of his head from one end of that Harlem apartment to the other. Pete Cullen's big black garrison belt,
which he wore with his green work pants, in which he
never seemed to do any work.

Connie the scapegoat who caught the brunt of it,
given he was the oldest, the only way Connie figured it.
Beat for his own failings and the failings of his siblings,
infractions large and small, depending on Cullen's state
of mind, and with it went the bond between the children:
Ruthie neglected to hang a wet towel up and Cullen took
the strap to Connie.

And his mother at the kitchen table, holding onto her
teacup with both hands, face turned away toward the
window.

Those months in Harlem occupied a lifetime's worth
of consciousness, a period his mind sifted over obses-
sively, attempting to puzzle out, decipher, glean, interpret
Pete Cullen's motives. Typical of children of alkies, Connie went far out of his way to make sense of and justify
somebody's heinous conduct, or better yet outright dismiss it as no big deal given the far harsher atrocities to
be found in the world, just pick up the paper. *It's not like
I'm waiting for a rice drop beneath a hovering helicopter,
and so who am I to complain?*

He came back to his body moving down the house's side
street, west of Madison, wondering how he arrived uptown. Did he walk? No. Okay, yes, he had taken the 6
train. Got off and, based on a *tap-tap* to his hip pocket,
picked up a pint from his spot on Lex. Or *someone* had
taken the train, *someone* picked up a pint.

"How you doing?"

Larry sat behind the wheel of the Datsun parked in the middle of the block, reading a paperback. He turned to look up at Connie on the sidewalk. "You drunk?"

"This what drunk looks like in California?" Connie said. "Let me ask you a question. Because I thought we were friends for a second there."

"We were friends, far as I'm concerned."

Connie slowly shook his head. "Nah, no way. Friends don't bullshit each other like you bullshitted me. I trusted you, Larry. I enjoyed talking to you."

"Me too!"

"Yes, but how can I believe you now?" Connie said, the betrayed wife. "Every word, tainted by deceit. There's no place for it in my life!"

"No place for what?" Larry said.

"The lies, the treachery!"

A man with a dog walked past Connie, keeping his head down, embarrassed to have eavesdropped on such intimate accusations.

"You used me," Connie said loud enough for the dog-walking man's ears, and they both laughed, Connie and Larry, and Connie lit a smoke. "I miss our times on the bench together."

"Me too," Larry said. "How do you think I feel?"

"Tell me," Connie said. "I'm listening."

"I'd rather be on *our* bench—it doesn't feel the same when I sit there by myself." Larry got out of the truck and leaned against the hood. "Give me a smoke."

Connie tapped one out, gave him a light.

Larry said, "I know you think I'm this two-faced person."

"Can you blame me? You flat-out lied. All you wanted was info on the family so you could get your pictures, to go ahead and do what, sell them to some cheesy-ass magazine? What the hell do you want to bother with this family for anyway, with your talent?"

"What do you know about my talent?"

"You showed me," Connie said, "on the bench."

"Did I?"

"That whole series on your brother Gerald."

"Oh, that's right!"

"All the shit you had to do to the house, you know, to make it livable."

"I remember," Larry said, his voice softening.

Black-and-white photographs of a young man in a wheelchair in and around a Craftsman house, in a section of Los Angeles Larry called Silver Lake. The pictures, unsentimental, nonmanipulative, took you to the edge but wouldn't indulge you. Their power had stunned Connie.

"This," he'd told Larry on their bench last fall, holding up the pictures, "is the real McCoy. You have an eye. A gift. Why are you looking at me like that?"

"How am I looking at you?" Larry said.

"Like I'm the only person who ever mentioned one good word about what you manage to capture with a camera."

"You might be," Larry said softly. "Just might be."

"Are you kidding me?" Connie said. "Don't you have any idea how good you are?"

Shot: Larry's older brother Donny picking Gerald up in his arms, both of them laughing, putting him into the shower, the new stall built to specs according to Gerald's limitations. Shot: Gerald on the porch, taking aim at a palm tree with a .357 Magnum, the fallen leaves in clumps at its base. Shot: Gerald on a daybed in the darkened living room, his body at its still-young age already atrophying, his extremities gnarling up.

Larry told Connie on the bench last fall that Gerald loved pussy, and dirty jokes, and that his brother had found a way to transmute his tragedy. "He never rolled over on himself." And that same day Larry had made what felt like a significant revelation to Connie: "Sometimes I think it's me who's paralyzed."

"How so?"

Larry stayed quiet, and Connie left it alone. And the real motive for Larry's presence got exposed soon thereafter, John pointing him out one day from the mouth of the service entrance.

"There he is."

"Who?" Connie said.

"The guy who's been taking my picture."

Henceforth Connie dismissed Larry as a charlatan, and everything about him grew suspect. Did Larry take those pictures of a guy in a wheelchair? Did he even have a brother named Gerald? And yet Connie also knew the connection was genuine, and even though he wanted to dismiss Larry as a fake, he really did find his photography truthful and compelling.

"You're a real artist, Larry," Connie said.

"Thank you."

"I mean it." Then: "The mother, by the way." Connie floated the information out with a thought to reconcile the friendship. "Down in Washington."

"Until when?"

"Tuesday."

"Not upstairs?"

"Just John and the governess."

"Okay."

"So you know."

"Appreciate it."

"Tell you the truth, if it was just the mother you were after, it wouldn't be a big deal. She's a big girl."

"When's Caroline coming back?"

Connie stared at him.

"What?" Larry said.

"You don't get it. What are you—"

"Why do you have to get on your high horse about it? They're just photographs."

"The kids, they need to be protected, and you don't seem to get that. Their privacy is sacrosanct," Connie said.

"Sacrosanct? Hate to burst your bubble, but those kids aren't all that innocent. Trust me, I got shots of them doing things I could have sold for a lot of money already, but I didn't, all right? I'm not looking to rat anybody out, okay—"

"Listen—"

"No, you don't understand! I have to make a living. Like you—you're a doorman, right? To pay the bills. I need to do the same thing. I'm not wealthy like these fuckers around here. I know how to use a camera and this work came up and I took it."

"Go ahead," Connie said, "be a prostitute."

"Listen to you—*sacrosanct*—who are you?!"

"Cut your own talent's throat if you want, but I'm telling you, don't take pictures of John. He's a friend of mine."

Larry gave a short laugh. "Friend of yours? You're a *doorman*. You polish the brass. You collect the garbage." Larry watched him. "I can't tell if you're serious."

Connie glanced around before he produced his pint and took a hit. "Let me ask: what would brother Gerald think about you betraying your talent like this?"

Larry locked eyes on him.

Connie said, "Take a picture, it'll last longer."

"Watch your step."

"Point a camera at the kid again and see what happens," Connie said, and as he crossed the street he held up a hand to stop an approaching car like he owned the block.

Connie gave Carlos a good break, letting him go at 2:35 p.m., and Carlos in gratitude slapped a fresh pack of Chiclets into Connie's hand.

"Thank you, Carlito."

"To keep you breath fresh."

No sooner did Connie get set up than the elevator rang. He rode up to fifteen and swung the door open onto the apartment's oval-shaped vestibule.

John stood there, a grin on his face. Next to him, leaning on its kickstand, a bicycle.

"Son of a. What the. Let me. Hang on a," Connie said. He hooked open the inner gate and stepped into the vestibule to take a three-sixty stroll around the bicycle beneath the oval-shaped chandelier. "Son of a b.i. biscuit. What's this, a—*Bianchi?*"

"Italian," John said.

"Check you out. Wait a minute now, this derailleur."

"I know."

"Ten-speed?"

"Yeah."

"Whoa. And this color's called what?"

"Cobalt. Octavio around?"

"Octavio's day off."

"He said he could help me put the rack on."

"Let me see." John handed it Connie; it looked to be a standard spring-hinged rack to be mounted over the rear wheel. "This is nothing. I'll help you."

"Got tools?"

"Got the keys to Octavio's shop." Considering the rack through its plastic, Connie said, "Looks like all we need is an adjustable, or maybe an Allen wrench. Come on."

John wheeled the bike onto the car with practiced caution, as the elevator's beautiful woodwork inspired a mindfulness. The strap of a tennis racket case cut across John's chest. Connie let the door collapse shut and dipped the lever.

"Son of a b.i. bitch. Ten-speed Bianchi, cobalt blue, you got to be kidding me. Mutt and Jeff know about this?" he said, referencing the Secret Service.

"What, can't I ride a bicycle?"

"Of course you can."

"Even my mother says it. I heard her talking to them. She said, *He's thirteen, he doesn't* have *an itinerary*."

"I hear you."

"I go to that stupid school, I play tennis, I get high, I ride my bike—*that's* my itinerary."

"You do more than that."

"Like what?"

"Play cribbage with your pal Connie."

John laughed. "Game of crib, Con, a little later?"

"Sounds good. Let's see what's what."

When they hit the basement Walter stood there.

"Hey Walter," Connie said.

"Hello," Walter said.

"Hi, Mr. Mezzola."

"Hello there," Walter said to John. To Connie: "What's up?"

"Putting a rack on the bike."

"Sounds good."

"Octavio's shop."

"Octavio's shop?"

"I mean—"

"First of all," Walter said, "if it's anybody's shop, it's management's shop. That shop, it belongs to the people who live here. Besides which, the tools in that shop—90 percent—my tools."

"I hear you."

"90, 95 percent. That shop, it's not Octavio's shop."

"He's a little territorial about it, it's true," Connie said.

"That shop is nobody's shop."

"I'll tell you," Connie said, "he knows I have a key but he doesn't like it a bit."

"If it's anybody shop, it's *his* shop," Walter said, pointing at John, who smiled, a little embarrassed. "That shop belongs to the tenants in this house. If it's anybody's shop, far as staff goes? Tell you the truth, that shop is *my* shop."

"I was going to say."

"Octavio's shop? I'm sorry."

"He does go around saying *my shop* a lot."

"He does!" John confirmed, chuckling.

"*My shop this, my shop that.*"

"Remind me to talk to Octavio," Walter said, making a small move.

"Need me to take you up?" Connie asked.

"Nah. Go ahead. Help him. I'll ring Stanley on the back. Got the key, you said?"

"Yeah."

"All right, good." Then: "Funny you have a key."

"I know. It *is* funny. But you know what?" Connie said. "Fuck Octavio."

Walter glanced at the rack in its plastic. "And do you know what you're doing?"

"Looks pretty easy. We'll figure it out."

"If you need help, say so."

"Thank you, Walter."

"Thank you, Mr. Mezzola."

"You're welcome."

Connie and John entered the shop and together put the rack on the bike without a problem. Connie grabbed a bungee cord among many hanging on a board, and John used it to fasten his tennis racket to the rack.

They walked out of the basement through the service entrance.

"Later, Con." John pushed off, swinging a leg over the frame. He reached back to double-check the racket was secure before powering up the ramp.

Connie watched the street from his below-grade vantage for signs of a flash, but none came.

Benjamin was on the front door at the doorman station. Connie stood just outside the idle west elevator down the length of the lobby. Benjamin was describing the plight of his drug-addicted daughter when a patrol car pulled up in front of the house. Benjamin read Connie's face and turned to the street, saying, "What's this now?"

John hopped out of the backseat of the patrol car and moved toward the entrance, just as Connie witnessed Larry come into view, his camera flashing once, twice—*flash-flash*. John grimaced and kept moving. Benjamin opened the door, telling Larry, "Enough with that," while the two NYPDs slowly got out, adjusting their gun belts.

John moved down the lobby. "Can you take me up, Con?" he said, heading into the elevator.

Connie saw the cops and Benjamin beneath the canopy, while the Secret Service agents, Ramey and Slovell, appeared as well.

"Con?" John said.

Connie turned and followed John onto the elevator.

"Somebody take the bike?"

"Yeah."

When the door swung open onto the vestibule, John said, "Come on, my room."

Connie secured the inner gate open with the hook and followed John down a maze of corridors, past a variety of interiors, the sight of which reminded him of the Met's French period rooms. A phone rang somewhere inside the vast apartment and a woman with a Spanish accent could be heard saying hello.

John's room had a schizophrenic design, the furnishings caught uncomfortably between two worlds—that of a thirteen-year-old boy's and that of the boy's mother, her touch evident in yet another chandelier, and valance curtains, and the room's stuffed chair and rococo moldings. The boy's contribution included an abundance of sporting goods scattered about. The space smelled like male adolescence—like somebody had been jerking off habitually. On the wall, a prominent poster of Muhammad Ali.

John plopped onto his bed and Connie took a seat in the stuffed chair.

"What happened?"

John folded his hands behind his head and stared up at the ceiling. "Motherfucker took my bike, that's what happened!"

"Tell me."

"I head into the park. Up the East Drive. I was going to go around. I was early for my lesson. Plus, I wanted to break the bike in a little, the brakes were squeaking. I'm peddling hard up the hill, and I reach down to change gears, and this guy comes stumbling at me."

"Stumbling?"

"Like maybe he's drunk or something. I had to brake hard, he's standing over me, and now with this smile I see he was faking. Holding my handlebars. Smiling at me."

"How old was he?"

"Nineteen. What he told me."

"You talked to him?"

"Yeah. He's asking about the bike, where I got it, how much it cost. Then he asks for a ride. I say no, I can't, I'm late. He keeps asking, I keep saying no, and finally he starts shaking the handlebars, he's banging the bike up and down, up and down, and he says, *Let's go! Let's go!* Like he's about to do something."

"Okay, all right."

"So I get off the bike. He gets on. I go to take the tennis racket at least, he says leave it there, leave it there. He's complaining the frame's too small for him. He's

just about ready to ride away, but then, like he forgot
something, he pulls me toward him and he checks my
pockets."

"Did he take anything?"

"No, I had nothing on me. He's says, *Where's your
bus pass?* I say, *I don't take the bus!*"

"All right."

"Motherfucker! Stupid fuck! I hope a truck runs him
over."

"Sure you're angry. Who likes to be robbed? Important thing is you weren't hurt."

"Fucking cocksucker."

"Listen to me now," Connie said. "You think you're
the only one who ever got mugged? I can't tell you how
many times I've been robbed. Yeah. On the train. Walking down the street. On the beach. Yeah, one time, in Co-
ney Island, I passed out in the sand, these two guys woke
me up to rob me! I said, *Why did you have to wake me
up? Why didn't you just take the shit?*"

John smiled a little.

"Yeah! They laughed too! This other time," Connie
said, "these two kids with a knife stole a can of baked
beans from me!"

"Baked beans?" John laughed.

"Right on 23rd Street. One can of beans. At knifepoint.
Unbelievable. What I'm saying, you're not the only one.
Honest to God, if they mugged me once they mugged me
twenty times. Congratulations. You lost your cherry."

"You're funny, Con."

Connie considered the poster of Ali and said, "He
started boxing right around your age."

"I love Ali."

"Do you know why he started to box?"

"Why?"

"Somebody stole his bicycle."

"For real?"

"Kid you not."

The governess—her name was Andrea—appeared in the doorway, her expression betraying a small shock at Connie's presence. She was South American. She was family.

"John, two detectives will be here in twenty minutes to talk to you."

"What for?" John said, annoyed. "I already told the cops everything."

"They're coming, and you have to speak to them," she said, appealing to the young adult in him.

Connie was on the fence about Andrea. She wore her Catholicism on her sleeve, used it like a shield. He feared she judged him from some secret place in her mind. Not so much as a hello on the elevator. Even John's mother said good morning and thank you. Generally he kept his distance, the vibe a strained neutrality.

To John, Andrea said, "Would you like a sandwich?"

John turned to Connie. "Want a sandwich, Con?"

"Not him, *you!*" Andrea said.

With a surprising outburst of emotion, John said, "He's my friend, Andrea!"

"He works here, John."

"So what? You work here too!"

Connie stood up. "Got to get going any case, thank you."

"Game of crib, Con, a little later maybe?"

"Definitely."

Andrea made a small show of stepping clear out of the doorway to let Connie pass.

By the time he descended back into the lobby, Connie's body was clicking with fierce resentment. One energized thought was really all it took. He headed for the sidewalk, where Ramey and Slovell, the two NYPDs, and Benjamin still convened beneath the canopy.

Connie yanked open the door. "Want to know the main problem?" he said to the cops. "The main problem." They looked at him, startled by his intrusiveness. "These two fucking humps right here," he said, pointing at Ramey and Slovell, who fell silent from the sudden force of his words. "Could give a shit about the kid. Say I'm lying."

"Hey," said the cop whose name tag read *O'Donahue*.

"Go ahead, say I'm lying."

"Con," Benjamin said.

"Let me break it down for you," Connie said. "That's not just any kid, all right, and these two are supposedly the quote-unquote Secret Service." Slovell glanced back at the Impala. "What, missing part of your ball game?" Connie said.

Slovell said, "Nothing but a drunk."

"Jig is up for the two of you, wait and see."

"All right, you're upset," O'Donahue said.

"He needs to be protected," Connie said. "Do I have to break it down for you? Do I?"

"No, you do not," O'Donahue said.

"Meantime, the kid gets robbed for his bike in the park, like who the fuck knows why he didn't get stabbed, follow me? And go ahead, tell me it doesn't happen, no—

but you know what, you know what, good in a way this
happened, 'cause both of your asses," pointing at Ramey
and Slovell, "getting shipped out to some cubicle, you
and you, supercilious sons of bitches, think I'm playing?
Watch and see, watch and—" Connie stopped. He looked
at the four of them, and he saw that all of them were
grinning, watching him as if he were an animal in a cage.
"What?"

"Go ahead," O'Donahue smiled, "you're doing good."

Connie sized them up. "Oh. Okay. All right. I get it,
I get it."

"What do you get?" Larsen, the other NYPD, said.

"Who's who and what's what vis-à-vis cahoots."

"What are you talking about?" Larsen said.

"A small taste," Ramey suggested to the cops, "of
what we put up with on a daily basis."

"Con," Benjamin said, "think I heard somebody ring."

"Cover for me," Connie said.

"Con—"

"Go ahead, Bennie, I got the front!" Connie said, and
Benjamin reluctantly headed into the lobby. The eleva-
tor had not buzzed: it was Benjamin's attempt to distract
Connie.

"Him I can trust," Connie said. "My union brother.
But you four right here? Now that I have your number?
Far as I can throw you. The four of you." Then, to the
cops only, Connie shook his head, saying, "Surprised at
you guys. Two fucking accountants, look at them, and
you got *their* back?"

Connie heard something, turned, and doubled over
with blinding surprise following the pop of a flash. Bent
over and sightless, Connie heard overlapping comments,

"Hey now, none of that now," from the cops and the agents.

"Anybody see a lens cap looks just like this?" Larry said, holding up a facsimile. This was Larry's technique, to shift attention away to something innocuous, a lost lens cap, say, and human nature being what it is, his disgruntled subjects would stop midobjection to help him look for a cap that was never lost to begin with.

Connie took his hands away from his face, his eyes recovering from the flash, and eyeballed Larry.

"See a lens cap just like this?"

"What did I say? I told you."

"Problem is," Larry said, "somehow you got the impression I take orders from you. I never listened to my mother, why would I listen to you?"

Connie stared at him. "No, I'll tell you—you're right," he said. "Absolutely right. Let me go and see what's what," and he turned to enter the lobby, going so far as to reach for the front door's handle, when he spun and sly-rapped Larry across the face. He boxed Larry's ear, grabbed and twisted it for a moment as well, and henceforth Larry would live with a minor case of cauliflower ear.

Larry, for his part, managed to push Connie away and unleash a camera from around his neck, the one without film, a 35mm German-made Exacta, gripping it like a baseball and bursting it down onto the side of Connie's head with harmful intention. All of this, Connie's sly-rap-cum-ear-twist, Larry's push-away and camera assault, took under two seconds, before the NYPDs managed to take a vague, lazy step toward them.

"Hell are you doing?" O'Donahue said.

"What's this now?" Walter said, approaching from the north.

"You the super?" Larsen said.

"Superintendent, yeah," Walter said.

"Can we talk somewhere?" O'Donahue said.

Larry turned and walked away.

"My office," Walter said. He looked at Connie, shook his head with disappointment.

Connie held the door open for the cops and the agents, who followed Walter into the lobby.

Trying to love somebody, that's your first mistake. You don't have the chops for love. They do studies on people like you, Con: if you didn't get it young you don't got it to give. It would take a special stroke of fortune for a life like yours not to be shot through to hell, nothing personal.

Connie felt a warm spot at the side of his head where Larry had clocked him, but his hand came away bloodless.

He stared down onto the elevator's floor, at a circular brass plate that read, *Otis*. He unfolded the *Daily News* from its spot and perused yesterday's stale headlines. All of it felt familiar: yesterday like today, today yesterday. Connie yearned for fresh sorrows.

The cops and Secret Service agents had come out from the back and walked past Connie like he no longer existed. Meanwhile, Walter had taken two detectives up to John's apartment.

Now the door to the back hall banged open. Stanley came toward him. Connie's face scrunched with mild confusion.

"Not even close to six."

Stanley relieved Connie for his break at six on Fridays as a rule, but the weird thing was, Stanley had on a doorman's uniform. He usually minded the car in his custodian's garb while Connie took his forty-five minutes.

"Doing what he told me," Stanley said.

"Walter?"

"Wants to see you."

"Okay. Okay." Connie moved toward the back with hesitancy. "So this right here's not my break?"

"I don't know, Con," Stanley said, "he just told me to put the uniform on and come up. He's in the office."

"All right, all right."

Connie pulled open the door to the back hall, then stopped in the doorway of the office.

"Yeah, come in," Walter said. "Sit down."

"What's up?"

"What's going to happen—Stanley come up?"

"Yeah."

"Sending you home, a one-day suspension."

"Suspension?"

"And this without pay."

"I don't understand."

"When's the next shift you're supposed to work?"

"What grounds?"

"Grounds?" Walter said. "How about the fact I saw you put your hands on the photographer? How's that for starters? Do you think you can work this house, throw punches, all at the same time, that what you think?"

"Walter, you didn't—"

"I saw enough to see what I needed to see!" Walter cried. "You punched him first, and regardless if what he's up to's right or not, beside the point."

"I mean," Connie said, "the issue at hand—"

"Can only look away so long, which I have done for a good while now is the truth, you drinking on the job and don't tell me you don't, what, am I stupid? Okay, but still, I thought, *Long as it doesn't get in the way, he's a good guy, got a family.*"

"Walter, the Secret Service, Ramey and Slovell, they're deflecting, don't you see? The kid got robbed in the park on their watch, that's the story, and so now it's my head gets served on a platter, is that the deal?"

"You don't stand in front of this house cursing out the Secret Service, you stupid or what? Get the fuck out of here. I'm going to write you up and suspend you. You make work for me, make work for everybody you pull this shit. Now, what you should do, go home and think if you still want to work this house, and you should thank me for not firing you on the spot. 'Cause believe me, Con, you can't see it, what I'm trying to do, save your job. Now go."

A one-day suspension was new on him. He'd been fired before in a variety of ways, dramatically and matter-of-factly, but a one-day suspension? Connie feared it sent a subtle message of shame he couldn't yet decode.

He stared into his locker, empty save for a black tie hanging on a rusty metal dowel. He never bothered to settle into a workplace like some of his coworkers who put up pictures of loved ones, calendars, or small mirrors, guys who actually used locks on their lockers. Making a comfortable space of any kind had never come easy for Connie. The times Maureen suggested sprucing up the apartment were received with numbing befuddlement, and he was bothered by it, thought it indicative of a self-annihilation he had battled his whole life. As a doorman he'd been inside many beautiful homes, but it wasn't just a class thing. In the projects people nested up their pads the best they could, and he even saw homeless people trying to trick out subway gratings with cozy touches.

He left by the service entrance without saying goodbye. The nods received from pedestrians on the street suggested he enjoy his break, while Connie in his cap and uniform held close the dirty secret of his suspension.

He wondered what had transpired in Walter's office, what got said about him in their little powwow. Four so-called officers of the law. Did they stand over Walter, saying, *Here's what you're going to do?* Walter's power of superintendence snatched from his hands.

Walter had stars in his eyes for the Secret Service, to Connie's mind. Ramey and Slovell had the most to lose and would want Connie out of the picture. Connie had their incompetent number. The two NYPDs seemed harmless enough, lost in the blue slumber of city jobs.

He walked his way downtown, deciding to not go gently toward termination. He was a dues-paying member of the doorman's union, 32B, and as such entitled to representation at arbitration. *There's a thing called labor law, a union contract. You don't kick me into the street without a fair hearing, that's not how it works, my friend.* South and west he meandered, taking in the architecture of carriage houses with invidious comparison.

He took the last swallow of his pint and gently left the bottle on a garbage heap rising like Mount Fuji over the rim of a can on the corner, Connie tippy-toeing away so as not to incite its collapse. He glanced around to see if anyone had benefited from his pantomime, and felt doubly embarrassed for: 1) hoping to have been seen; and 2) the fact that nobody *had* seen him.

Now he walked past a wall painted a shade of beige, which triggered a memory from last winter: moving down the stairwell of 466, leaving his apartment when nobody was around, as if his family had up and left him, heading out for a walk in the early evening, buttoning his overcoat, when an overwhelming feeling of alienation rode up on him and spooked him bad. He became unmoored and gripped the banister with both hands in fear of God knows what. And this shade of beige also called forth another time he came to consciousness after a fairly average run, awakening to the bedroom's morbid shadows from the streetlamps on Tenth Avenue. He had not wet the bed, as based on the dryness of his mouth and throat he was dehydrated from the booze and nicotine, his knuckles stained a toxic amber from the incessant smoking of cigarettes. When he came to he did not know if it was dusk or dawn, four a.m. or four p.m.—he never knew, not a clue after such runs assisted by cocaine or black beauties, capsules of speed fostering the ability to keep on drinking for up to a week's time. And this shade of beige cueing as well the bone-chilling loneliness that would follow such binges. Fearing not only the phone ringing but the *chance* the phone would ring. And there's always a chance it'll ring, so where does that leave you? The physical punishment the least of it, really, compared to the existential abandonment and terror that would rattle his limbic system in the wake of such runs. Like those moments in movies when the sound drains away. Captured by his own mind and no possibility of escape. He finally got up when his back couldn't take the bed any longer, drenched in sweat the dead of winter, the heat banging up through the pipes of the projects. Yes, it was four p.m., but of the second day: he'd slept the clock round after a five-day run. Hell, he felt certain, was painted a shade of beige.

He found himself moving through Times Square now, rife with deviance, past the downtrodden masses of the Deuce, trying to exact Buddhist detachment, nodding with equanimity to a woman in a bikini taking a smoke break outside a topless joint, before an apprehensive yearning in him harkened for shelter from the storm of humanity.

He used Port Authority as a transverse. It smelled of bus fumes and processed food. He did this with certain public spaces, performing a nonconsumer, noncommuter walk-through of Macy's, Gimbels, Penn Station, watching and mingling with people. He considered a quick cold one in Port Authority's bowling alley but decided to keep moving toward Grant's. He had a hankering for the familiar. *I should take the kids bowling*, he thought. *It's something families do together*. The one piece of advice he'd received as a kid came from his mother's brother, Uncle Paul: *Make your spares, the strikes will come*. Not bad, Uncle Paulie.

The fruit stands, the homeless, the century-old tenements, the human poetry of Ninth Avenue—all of it spoke to him in mournful tones as the sun got ready to clock out for the day.

He picked up a pint and crossed into Bums Park, and the thought of giving a look for his old discarded house key embedded in the street never entered his mind.

Connie went straight for Tommy Dunn on the bench

with an old-style diddy-bop to his walk, like back when they were kids.

"Tommy-Tom-Tom!"

"Who's that?"

"It's Connie, Tom!"

"Hey, Con!"

Connie shook Tommy's hand and sat down close, letting their legs bang together a bit. Tommy's family was from up the block too and they had all moved into the projects at the same time.

"How you doing?" Tommy cried.

"What are you doing, Tom?"

"I'm good," Tommy said, "doing good."

"Tom, now let me ask you something, I've been thinking about something. I'm curious now: exactly how the fuck does a guy lose a project apartment? I mean, you really have to go out of your way to fuck up in such a consistent and persistent manner for the city to kick you out of the projects—it's staggering to me you were able to succeed in doing such a thing. How did you manage it?"

Tommy looked at Connie, unsure, until he blinked, leaned back, stared up into the acorn-shedding trees of Bums Park, and let out a great roar.

"Ah, Con," Tommy said, "that's funny."

"You should know. Who was funnier than you? Listen, Tom," Connie said, producing his pint, "would it offend you very much if I had just a small taste?"

"*Offend* me?"

Connie cracked its seal, took a hit, and passed it to Tommy, who took a good swallow and handed it back.

"Thank you, Con."

Connie took another hit to let Tommy know he didn't

think he was contagious. "Tom, listen, I got to keep moving, but I've been thinking about you, and I'm keeping a good thought for you, and I wanted to stop, that's all."

"Glad you did, Con, for real."

Connie took another hit and slapped the balance of the pint into Tommy's hand, then reached into his pocket, peeled off a couple of bucks, and dropped them in Tommy's lap.

"Ah, Con, you sure?" Tommy said.

"Wish it was more," Connie said, walking away.

He cut a diagonal path through the projects toward Grant's, flashing on Tommy as a kid playing first base in Chelsea Park, circa 1962. His legendary stretch for the ball, a full split, scooping it up to just beat the runner. Tommy had developed a technique he saved for the most crucial moments of the most crucial games, wherein he could make it sound like the ball arrived before it did, and the first-base umpire, like Pavlov's dog, would respond to the bogus smack of leather Tommy produced with a fist-pumping call of *Oooouuuut!* The runner and first-base coach would go berserk as a poker-faced Tommy whipped the ball around the infield.

Connie moved through the yard of 466 when he spotted Maureen and knew the marriage was over. The trees of the yard in bloom and he knew. The green benches greener, juxtaposed against the gray of the concrete checker tables in the late-afternoon hour. Children played, grandmothers chatted in Spanish. Maureen stood at the entrance steps to 443, talking to a friend. The end of the marriage written on the small of her back. He could not see her face and he knew. The message of their dead marriage laid bare in her shoulders. He knew from her tone, echoing off the building back into the yard. Her body transmitted she was gone for good. He thought to stop and go to her but kept moving. She had gotten her hair cut and had those jeans on. The friend did a little thing with her lips and head, to which Maureen turned and saw Connie. They looked at each other a moment. Connie smiled sad, held up a simple hand. Maureen watched him, not angry, not fed up, just looked at him, before she turned back to her friend. Connie registered the desolate moment as a turning point of some kind when something made of glass containing a yellow liquid exploded at his feet. A mayonnaise jar filled with urine? Pickle brine? A cry of shock ricocheted across the yard. This, not a great habit certain project people possessed, mistaking their windows for trash receptacles. Connie kept moving as time spent looking up left you vulnerable and exposed. Several additional items bombed down around him, half a dozen eggs, followed by a muted thud. Connie spotted a head of iceberg lettuce rolling toward some bushes, abandoning a few outer leaves as it went.

Grant's Bar contained its typical cast of longshoremen and civil service workers, as well as those who worked the warehouses west of Tenth, from 14th to 34th. Whitey himself a one-man boilermaker factory behind the bar. They all stood and drank like men, except when they stood and cried like babies.

Whitey set Connie up. Connie banged back a shot and took a look around. *Is this ghetto of lost souls what I've given my life up for?* She had looked right through him, like a piece of glass, as if a stranger. *And maybe*, he thought, *I am.*

* * *

In Grant's he drank bats and balls for an hour. Dinner-time came and men headed home to their families. Con-nie ignored them.

He tried to shake the cynical thought that the world had revealed itself as false, this attitude seeming adolescent even to himself.

The ticker-tape theme noise of ABC's *Eyewitness News at 6* broadcast floated over the barroom, and there they were, stalwart coanchors Roger Grimsby and Bill Beutel on the thirty-two-inch Motorola, the dumbfounded box hovering on its jerry-rigged ledge.

Bill Beutel, a straight-ahead guy, seemingly devoid, unlike Grimsby, of shadow. Connie saw him on the street a few times up by Lincoln Center, a natty dresser, always a big hello.

"Mr. Beutel!" Connie once called out.

"Good to see you!" Beutel had waved back with his cigarette hand, so suave.

Connie never saw Grimsby on the street. Talk about attitude. Roger Grimsby. He got away with it because you knew he had furious love in his heart: the guy cared so damn much he had to hide it behind a wall of sardonicism.

The place had thinned out. Only Connie and Mr. Ri-ordan, an older wet-brain, remained. Whitey wiped down the bar in front of Connie and said, "Mind if I watch the news a minute?"

Connie knew the routine. Whitey went and grabbed the notched stick he used to manipulate the controls, turning up the volume.

Images appeared on the screen: a shot of the canopy, Benjamin retreating into the house, away from the camera, unwilling, apparently, to talk.

Beutel: "Occurred late this afternoon in Central Park."

"Turn it up—that's . . . turn it up!" Connie said.

Whitey worked the stick, and the volume shot up.

"Lower that damn thing!" Mr. Riordan said.

Connie held up a hand and said, "Shhh, shhh, Whitey, not too low, Whitey."

Roger Grimsby seemed disappointed with *Homo sapiens*. The whole human-race thing had grown tired, and the only way to protect himself against the moronic tales he peeled off the teleprompter required a deeply entrenched irony. The subtext of every story Grimsby reported, carried through his tone of quiet outrage, yielded a question: *Do you believe this nonsense?*

Connie knew Roger Grimsby was, as a baby, abandoned into an orphanage, which on Connie's darker days he found enviable. Familial tabula rasa sounded like paradise on earth, compared to the psychic truckload of atavistic bullshit Connie lugged around.

Beutel referred to actual copy before him, hot off the press: "Son of the late president has just a short time ago been accosted in Central Park. The thirteen-year-old, on his way to a tennis lesson, was mugged this afternoon. There are no reported injuries at this time, but his bicycle and tennis racket were believed stolen."

"Brand-new bike!" Connie cried.

Beutel: "John remains under the protection of the Secret Service, and as such there have been ongoing reports of disagreements between the agency and family."

Grimsby (ad-libbing): "This isn't the first incident."

Beutel: "That's right, Roger."

Grimsby: "The children, on occasion, have been something less than cooperative."

Connie: "Son of a bitch!"

Beutel: "According to the Secret Service, an itinerary for the boy is supposed to be submitted on a daily basis."

Connie: "Don't believe this!"

Beutel: "According to the report, the agents were un-aware that John had purchased a bicycle. As a rule, he takes a taxi to the tennis courts in the park, or receives a ride from one of the agents."

Connie: "Oh, that's bullshit!"

Grimsby: "The children's mother has made previous statements to the effect that she would like to see the children grow up in as normal an environment as possible, and the attempt to do so has made the role of the Secret Service, let's say, a more strenuous one."

Connie: "Son-of-a-bitch bastard!"

Mr. Riordan: "Shut the hell up!"

Beutel: "I'm sure we'll have more about this story on *Eyewitness News at 11*."

"Don't believe this," Connie said.

"What's the matter?"

"Like it's the kid's fault for getting robbed. Whitey, I work there, that's my building, I know the kid, a good kid!"

"All right, take it easy."

"Should see these guys—I deal with them day in, day out—and here you got two more jerk-offs bending over backward on their behalf."

"Calm down, Con."

"Ten-speed Bianchi, just got the damn thing. Do I have to spell out who the kid is?"

"To me?" Whitey said. "No, I know who—"

"This time the bike, next time what? Zero regard they

have. Like the assignment's above them, and so now they go and shoot an angle in the press: how difficult the children make it. They're kids, for Christ's sake! And they got the balls to float a story about how the kid's non-compliant, throw it back on the kid, when in fact those fucks don't want to do their job! No way. Not on my watch. Here, Whitey, break this for me." Connie pushed a dollar forward. "Think about it, what kind of outfit blames a *kid* to cover their own ass? And I'll tell you what: if they think for one second . . . You know what, now that I—fuck *Eyewitness News*. Give me some good old *Ten O'Clock News*. It's ten o'clock, Whitey, do you know where your children are?"

"CYO until seven thirty, then their mother picks them up," Whitey said, slapping down some change in front of Connie.

"Don't brag, Whitey." Connie downed his shot, picked up the change and his glass of beer. "So then I should do what, stand around, let this deception pass, and me, what, look the other way at the, what, expense of the kid?"

He stepped toward the phone booth and with peripheral vision caught the fleeting image of Arthur bouncing down Tenth Avenue out the window of Grant's, hopping off the ground, and the sight of his son stopped Connie midstep. He stared up into a corner of the barroom, where the tin ceiling met a water-stained wall, the glimpse of Arthur stunting his reverie of injustice. Seeing Arthur made him wonder what he was doing. He took a sip of beer and looked at the phone booth. *Who am I about to call?* And just as he remembered, an internal voice said, *Don't do it.* The voice, an agent of calm and reason, told him to say goodbye, go to the rooming house. *You're exhausted*, it said, *you haven't slept in fifteen years*. But Connie could not heed the voice, never could heed it. He went and unfolded the door of the booth and plopped down onto its shell-shaped seat. He picked up the phone, dialed 0.

"Operator Collins, how may I help you?"

"Yes, operator, good evening," and what a pleasure it was to receive help on the phone from a lady. "I'd like the number to WNEW, Channel 5, the television station, if I could. The *Ten O'Clock News*. Yes, operator, that's correct. Thank you."

Whitey wiped down a section of the bar across from the booth while Connie held on, playing with the door, searching for the exact spot on its track which ignited the booth's light and fan.

"Yes," Connie said into the phone, giving Whitey an outlandish wink. "The *Ten O'Clock News* program, specifically, operator. Pardon me? Well, let's see, all right. Fine, let's give the news desk a try. That would be just great, thank you. Yes, yes, I do indeed."

Whitey screwed up his face as Connie placed a dime in a slot and the phone accepted it with a pleasant jingle.

Connie closed his eyes and saw the operator sitting before her patchwork board of cloth-wrapped wires. She was short, a little plump, wore glasses and clear nail polish, and for some reason had never married. She had managed to forego carnality and live the contented life of a telephone operator.

He lit a cigarette, took a swallow of beer, leaned back in the booth, ready to don the necessary persona to get what he wanted.

"Yeah," he said, sitting up, "this the news desk? All right, good. Well, chances are I got a story for you. Pardon me? Go ahead. Yeah, well, first of all, who am I speaking to? Okay. Fine, fine. But listen, do me a favor: speak directly into the mouthpiece, 'cause it sounds like you dropped the phone into a bag of potato chips. Well, okay, okay, the nutshell's what happened this afternoon in Central Park to the kid. Yeah, I saw it, but they got it wrong, entirely wrong. Correct. All right, I'll tell you how I know, but do me just one favor and don't bullshit me and don't waste my time. I work in the house. Correct. Correct. No, I, look, bottom line's I got proof, proof, follow me, the kid's not being protected, that's the story, story behind the story, not what Channel 7's throwing up there, which, believe me, got spoon-fed, if you follow my gist. Exactly. The blow-by-blow. Are you kidding me? Let me count the ways. Right now? 25th and Tenth. Huh? Grant's Bar it's called. Southeast corner. Well, yes, but you have to tell me."

"What are you doing?" Whitey said.

"Have to tell me exactly."

"Don't have them come around here," Whitey said.

"All right, fine, just be sure, and then I'll go ahead— I'm in a doorman's uniform. That's what I'm saying. Now you're learning! All right, when you get here." He hung up and stepped out of the booth.

"What did you do?" Whitey said.

"They're coming to interview me in half an hour."

"Where?"

"Here. At the bar. Or in the back, what do you think?"

"I don't want cameras in here."

"Why not?"

"What if Gene doesn't want it?"

"Aw, Whitey, fuck Gene. Honest to God. Gene's not here. Gene's never here. If Gene gave a shit, *Christ*, Gene don't even come around to pick up the bag of money anymore. Speaking of which, look at this place, all the cash dropped in here, can't slap some paint on the walls, and you're worried about *Gene*? Whitey, please."

The interview Connie gave to WNEW-TV made the *New York Times*, the interview itself becoming news for reasons he could not envision. Hundreds of viewers called the station with complaints that the report was the "exploitation of an unfortunate person"—meaning Connie— while the piece in the *Times* did not address the performance of the Secret Service, or John's mugging, but rather the ethics of a television station which may have taken advantage of a disturbed drunk in a bar, and the station's defense of its reporting. My God, people cried into their phones, to abuse such a man in such a manner, shame on you, WNEW.

It was one of those things that demonstrates television's tentacles. Maureen and Arthur and Steven saw it. Three of Maureen's brothers saw it. Walter and his wife and half the guys on staff saw it (as well as three influential members of the board). At the rooming house Susan saw it with Justin and David, prior to the three of them stepping out to a midnight meeting. John and the governess and the mother saw it, the mother having flown up from Washington. Arthur's friends saw it, becoming ever more eager for their next stairwell sounding session.

A non-logoed, wood-paneled boat of a station wagon had pulled up outside Grant's, the sun having set just long enough to call it night. As the crew started to dewagon themselves, Connie ducked into the bathroom to take a leak, unsure how to play it. Should he not be conscious of the cap's angle on his head? Should he, once the cameras roll, remove the cap, thoughtfully feeling its rim between thumb and forefinger, considering each question posed to him with contemplative modesty?

With a wet palm he had jabbed at the stainless steel stem of the Borax dispenser, letting its coarse crystals drop and dissolve in his hands. He splashed water on his face, turned and yanked blindly for a fresh section of towel. At the mirror he made one last cap adjustment before heading out, an insane swagger of authority in his walk.

"There he is," Whitey said.

A man introduced himself, and Connie hid his disappointment: they had sent a lightweight. The guy tried too hard, going for a Gabe Pressman–like effect, an everyman in shirtsleeves, but couldn't quite pull it off. He had yet to acquire the gravitas and bona fides, and his assignments to date, as Connie recalled, didn't have much import. The reporter, whose name was Harriman, hammered on points in his stories that were common knowledge like they were profound revelations, the pieces no more than fluff.

"Let me ask," Connie had said. "I mean, how did they decide to send you?"

"It's an important story," Harriman said. "We're talking about the president's only son. Not just another mugging in the park, not any kid's bicycle."

"Got that right."

"The desk put the call out and we jumped on it, because what happens to those kids has serious implications for the future of our country. They are our future is how I look at it, if only, you understand, symbolically."

And Connie had thought, *Huh. This could be his breakthrough assignment, and the guy will look back fondly at the role I played in his career jump. I'll see him here and there over the years and remind him I knew him when.*

"Give us a couple minutes to set up," Harriman said.

"Where do you want to do it?" Connie said.

The producer, a woman with long blond hair and angular features, said, "How about right where you're standing?" before she slid into the phone booth and unfolded its door.

Besides Harriman and the woman, there were two crew members, camera and sound, moving equipment around.

"Ripped," the sound guy whispered. The camera guy saw Connie making the thinnest stabs at sobriety, but despite the absence of slurred speech, his alcohol intake had circled back on him, and he was plowed.

Connie had no on-camera experience, possessing only an autodidact's amount of PR guile from what he read on the fly, and he was practicing a nonchalant pose of integrity against the bar when the crew banged on the lights.

"Whoa," he said, "little on the bright side."

"Want a minute to adjust?" Harriman said.

"Let's go for broke," Connie said, shaking out a smoke.

The camera guy gave a hand signal he had given a thousand times, and the reporter, microphone in hand, started talking.

"Sir, what is your name?"

"Cornelius Sky."

"By the way," Harriman said, "some of this we'll cut, so don't worry."

"I don't want to tell you your job," Connie chuckled, "but don't cut it all."

"It's great you have the uniform on."

"Thank you."

"Where do you work?"

Connie stated the address.

"Is this the residence of the former First Lady and her children?"

"Correct."

"And you called the station yourself, did you not?"

"Correct."

"Why did you call us?"

"Tell you what, I was watching *Eyewitness*—"

"Don't mention another station by name," Harriman said.

"A report about the kid getting mugged in the park. And they made it out like it was the fault of John himself."

"How did they do that?"

"He got robbed in the park, somebody took his bike, brand-new ten-speed Bianchi."

"That's the story so far, yes."

"Now, why would they want to slant it in such a way that they go and try to put blame on the kid, follow me? They made the story out like the kid's always running away."

"Eluding," Harriman said.

"Very good, eluding," Connie said. "When in fact the

Secret Service, the two guys assigned to protect the kid, they don't give a shit."

"Don't curse."

"Could care less, that's my main point, why I called you guys down here—that's the story, the story behind the story. We're talking about the president's son, correct? Kid loved that bike, could see it in his eyes."

"In what ways have the Secret Service not done their job?"

"Surprised nothing's happened sooner, 'cause what they do, sit there in the shade, eat buttered rolls, drink coffee from the Greeks, and then to have the gall to turn around and blame it on the kid? The family doesn't present the itinerary, they say—but the kid doesn't have an itinerary, doesn't *want* an itinerary, he's thirteen years old. Whitey, please," Connie said, holding up an empty glass. "Sit there in their sedan, their buttered rolls, I kid you not. Only time they come into the house, to use the facilities, if you follow me. Concerned is my point, extremely concerned." Connie half turned his back to the camera with polite discretion and drained a shot. "With the kid's interest in mind, first and foremost, why I called. I know all about people not saying boo on a kid's behalf. But not on *my* watch. As a doorman I do all I can, but what can I do as a doorman? They should not put it on the kid like it's his fault, that's all. Let the kid be a kid, and you be the Secret Service. What is the job description when you think about it? You would think part of the job's to, you know, check on the comings and goings in and around the house, no? What's the word?"

"Background checks? Vetting?"

"Exactly," Connie said. "Very good. Part of the Secret

Service's job, you would think. Yet everybody and their mother comes and goes, no questions asked. Like part of my job description: to open doors, get cabs, hold packages, deliver the mail, buff the floors, polish the brass, who knows what else. Be of service to the tenants the best I can. That's my job description. What's your job description? To get the truth, right? What's *their* job description? To eat buttered rolls, drink coffee, not move a muscle? You tell me."

"How much have you had to drink today?" Harriman said.

"Me? How much? I've had a few beers, but really I have no reason to count."

"And a few shots?"

"Perhaps," Connie said. "This is a drinking establishment. Why do you ask? It seems a little off the subject at hand."

"I want to know who I'm talking to," Harriman said. "You talk about background checks. I need to know the information you're giving us is accurate and valid."

"Fair enough, fair enough." Connie removed his cap and showed it to Harriman. "You see what it says right here? Want the camera to get a shot of this?" Around the cap's band, in cursive stitching, the house's address.

"Fine," Harriman said, "you work in the building, let's assume that's true, but making accusations against a venerable government agency should not be taken lightly."

"It grieves me, you kidding? But I should do what, put the agency's reputation before the protection and safety of the kid? You tell me. How venerable's that?"

"Of course not."

"This time a stolen bike, next time what, follow me?

And don't tell me people don't get stabbed in that park for a funny look, forget a Bianchi. Think about it: president's son stabbed to death in Central for his bicycle. How's that for a story—would you like to cover that one?" They stared at one another a long moment. "Let me ask you something," Connie said to Harriman. "Did you have a bike when you were a kid?"

"Yes, I did."

"I bet you did. And I bet you had a father too."

"I did."

"Good for you," Connie said. "Good for you."

"What about yourself?"

"Me? Sure, I got my hands on a bike or two."

"Did you have a father?"

"Did I myself personally have a father?"

"Yes."

"Good question."

"Did you?"

"I would say yes and no."

"Yes and no?"

"In the sense he died at a certain point."

"I'm sorry."

"That's okay."

"When?"

"When?"

"How old were you when he died?"

"He died when I was nine years old."

"How did he die?"

"How did my father die?"

"Yes."

Connie looked at him, chuckled in a sad manner. "He put his head in the oven."

The producer quietly opened the phone booth, stepped out, and moved closer to the scene, next to the sound guy, who held the squirrel-tailed boom just out of frame.

"Your father committed suicide."

"Yes," Connie said. "Yes he did. Turned the oven on and took our youngest brother with him. Though Edward's death was by all accounts unintentional, that my father assumed himself alone in the apartment at the time. This should be stated for the record, I would say."

The crew and the producer exchanged looks, unsure what, if anything, they were getting.

"That must have been difficult for you, as a child," Harriman said.

"How so? Whitey!" Connie said, holding up his glass. Then back to Harriman, "Go ahead, I'm curious to hear your take."

"To lose your father at the age of nine. By his own hand. You must have felt a terrible loss."

"Yes and no, yes and no," Connie said, with some drunken reflection. "Truth be told, prior to his death, he was basically a blur in any case."

"What do you mean, blur?" Harriman said.

Connie spelled it: "B-L-U-R. Come on, you know what *blur* means. And you have concerns about *my* drinking! Whoa. Now that son of a bitch could put it away!"

Several men had entered, customers, regulars who clustered together down the bar to watch and listen.

"You mentioned the number of people that come and go. Do you think the security the building provides is sufficient?"

"Well, the staff of the house, it doesn't have the

whatchamacallit, wherewithal, the resources, to check the background of every guest, deliveryman, contractor. That's the job of the Secret Service, wouldn't you say? And how many more times will they drop the ball is my main point."

And as he spoke Connie again considered the true source of his disdain, if it had more to do with Francis Ramey reminding him of the kid who foot-tapped his desk for the month he spent as a ninth grader at Cardinal Hayes.

Only God holds the list of secret motives.

"Proof," the producer woman said, sotto voce, to Harriman.

"You said on the phone you had proof," Harriman said. "What proof do you have for your claim?"

"You want proof?" Connie said.

"We need it, we—"

"All right, all right, here's the deal, I'm catching up to you. You talk about staff, talk about people coming and going. Okay, now I know personally, personally for a fact, that those kids have been left alone many times with people, let's say, with problems, an official record of problems, let's say."

"In the building."

"Correct."

"What kind of problems?"

"What kind of problems? People, let's say, with a history of . . . all right, let's call it mental illness for lack of a better way to express it."

"Are you talking about a tenant in the building? A member of the staff?"

"No. Yes, staff."

"A member of the family's staff?"

"No, no, there's only—"

"The building staff?"

"Correct."

"Who is it?"

"An employee, let's say."

"What's his name?" Harriman said.

"His name?"

"Yes."

Connie looked at Harriman a moment, then smiled strangely. "It's me. Me myself." He snorted, perversely enjoying the look of confusion on Harriman's face. He shook out another Camel and lit it with the Zippo's wild flame. "See what I'm saying? As an example of so-called proof, I say this to you. So if somebody like me, for example, who's been to Bellevue himself, who they say has a small history of mental illness of some kind, a nervous disorder, call it what you will, if someone like me, on paper, has access to the kids, the question then becomes who *else* has access? Follow my point? Is it not a reflection of what we're talking about, a laxity, let's say?"

"You've spent time as a mental patient at Bellevue?"

"Correct."

"Why?" Harriman said. "I mean, under what circumstances?"

"First time I thought I was going to kill myself, and my wife walked me over, pregnant with our first son, and they went ahead and admitted me just to play it safe."

"The first time? And then? I mean . . ."

"The second time I'm not sure is the truth. They found me nude behind the wheel of a stolen Dodge Charger on 8th Street. What a mess. But the main point, vis-à-vis how lame, or forget lame, nonexistent, the background checks."

"And you, yourself, have been alone with the children?"

"Sure," Connie said. "Many times. The elevator, whatever. Part of the job. Which is my point."

Harriman adjusted his body, lifting both feet off the ground slightly, one at a time, as if to reset himself. "And you, yourself, do you ever feel as if you might be in danger of hurting the children?"

"Hah?"

They exchanged looks, and Connie thought he saw something in the other man's eyes. Harriman showed teeth, a dark grin in service to the scoop he could taste, his face flushing like a bright bird of prey.

"You say you've been to Bellevue as a patient."

"Right, right."

"That you have a history of mental illness."

"I'm listening to you."

"And you, you called us yourself, because you're concerned about John and—"

"Correct."

"And I'm asking you, directly, if you have ever felt you could possibly hurt them, yourself."

"Me? Hurt them? I—"

"Have you hurt them already?"

"Hurt them already?" Connie stared at Harriman, as the meaning of his questions washed over him, and the stark camera lighting brought into relief a look of profound and naked disturbance.

"I . . . Wait now." He half turned, reached for the bar.

"Is that why you called us, Mr. Sky? To protect the children?"

"In what? How?"

"Protect them from yourself?"

"I . . . I mean. How would I hurt them?"

"I don't know! You tell me!" Harriman demanded. "You're the one who called the station. You're the one with the history of mental illness. You're the one with access to the children. You're the one who has spent time with them alone."

"I . . . You."

"Have you hurt them?"

"I called because."

"Answer my question: have you hurt the children?"

"Hurt them? Hurt them?" Connie said. "I would never hurt them, never, not ever in a million years. I love those kids too much, I love those kids. I could never hurt a kid." And he started to weep.

A man at the end of the bar said, "Ah, Christ."

"I could never hurt them. Can you . . . can you shut it now?" Connie said, gesturing feebly at the lights and camera. "How could you? To ask me such a thing . . . Your implication," Connie said. "I could never hurt those kids. I love them too much. That's why I called you, that's why I called you, to make sure they're protected, that no harm comes to them."

"Would you like them to be protected from *you?*" Harriman said. "Is that why you called?"

Connie stared at him a moment, aghast. "My God, oh my God," he said. "To be so accused. To be so accused," and he turned away, hid his face against his arms, folded down onto the bar, and he wept loudly, shoulders bobbing.

The producer said to the cameraman, "Push in, Joe. Hold on him," and the cameraman did, they all did, the entire bar, Whitey and customers and crew, they all held on Connie as he soaked the sleeves of his jacket, the only sound in Grant's his mournful cries.

"Good," she said, "let's wrap."

Harriman turned from Connie like rolling off a whore, and as the crew started to strike the set, Whitey brought Connie a fresh boilermaker.

"Come on, Con."

Connie hid his face a long while, until he heard the crew making its exit, the producer calling out an empty "Thank you!"

This unofficially marked the run of Connie's tears. Between jags, he could go for years without shedding a solitary drop, shuffling the streets of Manhattan all dried up. He thought, *Go ahead and let it all out, you big baby*. He slowly took a peek forward and saw the boilermaker on the bar before him in close-up. He grinned and stood up straight.

"Thank you, Whitey!" he said, downing the shot. Then, generally, to the bar: "Did I hang myself out to dry or what?"

"You sure did," Shorty Cordero said.

"Why do they call it the fourth estate, does anybody know?"

"My God," PhD Roy said, "what on earth did they do to you?"

"Took me to the cleaners, Roy. Railroaded me like nobody's business."

"He called the station himself," Whitey said.

"My heart goes out to you," Butchie Morelli said. "I hate to see a man reduced to tears like that."

"For all the world to see," Spivey Curtis said.

"He said they fix things when they edit. Maybe they'll cut my crybaby routine, you think?" Connie said.

"I wouldn't count on it," PhD Roy said. "If they use any of it, they'll use your emotional outburst. I came in just when you started to break down, and the look in that reporter's eye."

"I told you not to call."

Two hours later they watched the broadcast huddled together at the bar. Whitey used the notched stick to get Channel 5 on, just as a tone signal beeped and a voice-over inquired: "*It's ten o'clock: do you know where your children are?*"

As it turned out, WNEW attempted to use Connie's interview to its full advantage, though karmic justice made it backfire on them just as it had on Connie, with Harriman and the producer, Megan O'Rourke, receiving public reprimands. The outcry helped Connie's ego recover from the most severe kind of humiliation: being cross-examined by a TV reporter about harming children, and, left unspoken but darkly implied: harming them sexually. *Alone. On the elevator. Answer me! Did you?*

Connie's heart vexed something awful. If the accusations were so outlandish, so baseless, so devoid of truth, why then did they hit him with such force? Why did he not laughably dismiss the accusations at the outset? Why was he so suggestible as to his being such a heinous and reprehensible human being?

"Coming up," John Roland, the *Ten O'Clock News* anchorman, kept saying, "an exclusive interview with a doorman employed at the residence, regarding the mugging of the president's son, which occurred earlier today."

They had teased the story out before each break. Finally, at 10:54 p.m., they'd aired the interview, and the men at the bar had gathered around Connie.

He'd watched with detached wonder, knowing what was coming yet experiencing it as if for the first time, while the men got caught up in the scene's trippy recursion: watching an interview filmed in the exact spot they stood. There, Connie up on the Motorola, and next to them, Connie in his doorman's uniform. And at the moment Connie started to break down, a few guys at the bar snickered, and Connie himself chuckled, and before long everybody roared at the sight of him collapsing into tears. The men indulged their fit of hysterics and slapped at each other. Whitey reached for a clean towel and held it to his face, and with his other hand protected his crotch, as if to prevent his balls from shooting away from his body. Connie never saw Whitey laugh so openly, so hard.

ARTHUR AND HIS FRIENDS, REDUX

In Arthur's eighth grade English class at IS 70 earlier that day, the kids could tell Mr. Silverstein was tired. They liked him, the man could teach, but it was a Friday of a long year and everybody in the building was ready for summer to break.

They were studying words that contained the *-ism* suffix. Mr. Silverstein had asked them to find such words in their dictionaries, and to use the words in sentences in their vocab tablets.

Arthur had written: *Masochism hurts like it should.*

Now he searched the late-night stairwells for Rennie, Errol and Joey, Albert, and Michael. The second floor of 288, the fourth floor of 443, the eighth floor of 446, the fifteenth floor of 428. Nobody liked 415: an incredibly large, out-of-control, mixed-race family lived in 415, speculation running as to the exact number of kids, fourteen or sixteen, even eighteen, with people assuming some sort of foster-care scam, and all told they messed the building up. Even in the projects there was always one building that other buildings got on their high horse about and ostracized. The housing cops were always double-parking outside 415 in response to some baby almost drowned in a tub, or a kid busted up from a fall down the shaft.

Arthur checked the ninth floor of 427 and there they were, smoking and spitting. He banged opened the stair-well door and said, "Housing," mimicking the baritones of NYCHA workers.

"Been praying for your ass to show up."

Arthur got settled, started to smoke and spit.

"Fuck's your father going on TV for, that drunk bastard?"

"He looked like a maniac, for real."

"Least my father don't walk around with a pocket-book like your faggoty-ass father."

"Seriously," Joey added, "I never got the sense he was so ignorant of a man." Joey's delivery was good.

"I'll never look at your father the same again," Ren-nie said. "Before going on TV he was just one more drunken-ass bum. Now I have a special pity in my heart for you and Stevie, Artie, and your sexy-ass mother, who I still want to fuck, by the way."

"Me too."

"Speaking of mothers," Arthur said.

"*It's ten o'clock: do you know where your drunken crybaby father is?*"

"*It's ten o'clock—*"

"He's in Grant's Bar giving a drunk-ass interview be-fore he breaks down into his beer."

"Before he starts bawling like a drunken bitch baby."

"Imagine your mother winding up on TV," Arthur said to Rennie. "Or your little bald-headed Jew father?" he said to Joey and Errol. "Or your little spic father?" he said to Albert. "Think about it, Albert," Arthur said, "your father fixes flats on Tenth Avenue. That's like half a step above a panhandler."

"Closer to a tie."

"So?" Albert said, caught off guard. "So?"

"And you know what else I get a kick out of?" Arthur said, experiencing the freedom of those to whom a worst-case scenario has actually transpired. His father went on television and made an idiot of himself, topping it off with one of his breakdowns. It left Arthur with nothing left to hide. "Albert, you show up like your father's off limits. Don't act all sensitive when I mention your little tire-changing bitch father, you faggot."

Some good laughs shot up the stairwell.

"Fixes flats, yeah, but he don't call the *Ten O'Clock News* to come and make a big ass of himself."

"'Cause your father still don't speak English."

"Albert's father would have to call the Spanish channel," Errol said.

"Telemundo," Joey said, and the word got a laugh.

"Your father makes a bad alcoholic look good, that's how bad your father is. Your father should head straight back to Bellevue and stay there where he belongs," Albert said.

"Oh shit, that's right, I forgot the Bellevue part!"

"They could still let him wear his doorman uniform in the halls up there, like a cop for the crazy people."

"Did you see your father on TV, Artie?" Rennie said conversationally.

"Yes I did, Rennie, thank you for asking," Arthur responded, which got a laugh for delivery.

"Okay, okay, so now what kind of idiot squeals on himself like that?" The kids made noises of concurrence. "There's somebody in the building who's crazy, your father says. And then he goes, *It's me*."

"Who is that stupid?"

"Not the stupidest criminal on *Perry Mason* would pull that shit, and here comes Mr. Sky on the *Ten O'Clock News.*"

"Setting himself up with no help from nobody."

"One thing to be a drunk, one thing to be crazy, but even crazy drunk people ain't that stupid."

"Dopey-ass motherfucker."

"I see him walking around, one of the top like two or three most terrible alcoholics in the whole projects. I see him curled in a ball on the floor, sleeping it off down in Penn Station. I see him pissing in phone booths in the middle of the day."

"I saw him drunk right off his ass on the train. I said, *Please, God, don't let him see me,* and he's not even my father, so I can imagine, Artie, how you and Stevie must feel."

"People stepping over his ass, fucking rush hour."

"I hate to see Mr. Sky drunk in Penn Station. Something about it breaks my heart," Joey said wistfully. "Went to a Knicks game and there he was, sprawled on the floor like it was his bedroom, and he had clearly urinated upon himself."

"Seriously, Artie: your father is a real fucking bum. What are we going to do about this?"

"*The crazy employee in the building is me,* he says. *Yes,* he says, *that's correct, I have been locked up in Bellevue.*"

"And, ho shit, Artie, I didn't know your grandfather committed suicide."

"That's a whole other story."

"Let's discuss that, shall we?"

"That shit is contagious, they say."

"When do you plan on killing yourself, Artie?"

"I could see you killing yourself, Artie, one of these days, that makes sense."

"But only after Mr. Sky kills himself."

"Then it's your turn, Artie."

"Then what I'll do, marry your mother and become Stevie's stepfather."

"Artie's grandfather put his head in the oven."

"Do you ever see your father acting funny around the stove, Artie?"

"Don't leave your father alone in the kitchen, Artie. If he's hungry, get his ass some takeout, but whatever you do, don't let him congregate anywhere near that fucking stove."

"Daddy, why is your head in the oven?"

"Daddy, why are you on your knees in front of the oven with the door open?"

"I'm fixing something, son."

"Yeah, right, Dad. Since when do you fix things around here? All you do is drink your ass off."

"Artie, would you thank your father for me? That's the best shit I saw on TV in a long time."

"Poor Mrs. Sky. When you think about it."

"All she wanted was a decent life."

"She thought she was marrying a man, not a drunk-ass baby in a doorman's uniform."

"Your grandfather killed himself. Mr. Sky is doing his best to kill himself. Artie, what about you?"

"I'll be missing you, Artie."

"Imagine if Artie was dead?"

"Artie, will you leave me your hockey shit so I can sell it to one of the white boys?"

"Artie, please don't kill yourself, not yet. We still got some good years to goof hard on your ass."

"Plus," Joey said, "I have plans to get next to your mother, and I'm going to need your help."

"That bitch is still so fine to me."

"It's common knowledge I want to fuck your mother, Arthur."

"Me too."

"Could we pull a train on your mother, Artie, you think?"

"How those dungarees hug her ass just right."

"Just right, so very tight."

Arthur was laughing, letting the spit fall out of his mouth, as the kids looked at him with love and affection.

"Would you happen to know, Arthur, if Mrs. Sky enjoys oral sex?"

"Say it plain: does your mother like to suck dick, Artie?"

"I can answer that," Errol said.

Out of the blue, Albert, who had grown quiet, said, "My father fixes flat tires, so what?" He looked about to cry.

"This guy!" Joey said. "So sensitive all of a sudden!" and they all laughed.

"*It's ten o'clock: do you know where your dead grandfather is, the one who died by suicide?*"

"*Ten o'clock: do you know where your little flat-fixing father is?*"

"Least he didn't put his fucking head in the oven."

"*It's ten o'clock: don't nobody light a match!*" Michael said, and a silence fell upon the stairwell.

"Every time you open your mouth, shit comes to a standstill, you purple-face bitch," Rennie said. Michael had a birthmark on the side of his face and neck, a dark crimson blotch, vaguely shaped like the United States of America.

"*It's ten o'clock: do you know where the man who walks and talks like a faggot, and carries a purse, and has a faggot son with purple on his face is?*"

"It's a satchel," Michael said.

"Fuck you," Joey said, "it has a strap."

"A clasp," Errol screamed.

"Which makes your father, ipso facto, a queer."

CHAPTER FIVE

NOW THAT HE WAS OFFICIALLY KICKED OUT, and had a room of his own, it worried him in a strange new way to come to in Penn Station. Something called him to this passageway, low-ceilinged, lit by creepy fluorescents, herding with sorrowful purpose thousands of LIRR commuters to and from their trains, a hard-tiled corridor in desperate need of stripping by someone just like Connie, and the spot's apparent draw alarmed him.

People loomed, hurried by. He got a few double takes because of the uniform, he thought, but it was the pathos stitched into the features of his face. He in turn watched the commuters, tried to consider how they did it. So much gumption in their collective gait, the alacrity of their comings and goings signifying such import. *Are you serious? Are you for real?* A terrible chasm of mental disease, a horrid free-floating aura of meaninglessness took him over, and for a long frightening moment scrambled all visual reference code into gibberish. To everything his eyes landed on—a folded beach chair tucked beneath a freckled arm; the tiny putty-colored wheels of a baby stroller; the baton of a cheerleader in frantic search of a team to root for—to all of it his mind fearfully pleaded, *Why? Why?*

He braced for movement, using the wall against his back to rise up, then again using it to rise down to retrieve his cap, before making his way out of the station.

He saw Shane tossing sawdust from a red bucket out onto the Blarney Stone floor, his gestures familiar to any sidewalk pigeon feeder, the tossing of the sawdust a benediction onto the space. He tapped on the glass of the door with a nickel. Shane came and opened up on Connie's behalf, not for the first time, Shane good that way, locking up behind him. He brought a water glass filled with whiskey and a pitcher of beer to Connie, sequestered in a back booth.

Connie grabbed his own wrist to guide and steady the hand that held the glass to his mouth. He didn't care for the word *shakes*, finding it melodramatic: a half case of the jitters described it well enough.

Shane appeared from the kitchen, went and slid a stainless steel tray into a smoky hole at the steam table, before coming over to Connie with a cup of coffee of his own, and took a seat.

"You all right then?"

Connie closed one eye with doubt.

"We saw you on the television last night," Shane said.

"My attempt to set the record straight."

"My wife was concerned when I told her I knew you," Shane said, adding, "your well-being, Con, that's all."

"Yeah, I made an ass out of myself."

"Making an ass of yourself is one thing. Be sure you take care now."

"Thank you, Shane."

"Some breakfast then?"

The smell of the bacon from the kitchen made him

nauseous. Saying it as a throwaway line, Shane once told him a true Irishman never enjoyed his drink more than his food, but Connie was not Irish, he was American, born in French Hospital on 30th Street, December 4, 1942, the same hospital where Babe Ruth was treated before he died. Six-year-old Connie tugged at his father's sleeve, trying to learn what floor the Babe was on in French— they heard it on the Philco—and what floor he and his siblings were born on, wondering if he and the Babe had shared the same room. His father had no answers, only a look of strange astonishment, Sammy thrown by Connie's inquiries. *Was Patty, was Eddie, was Danny, was Ruthie born in French, Dadda? What floor, Dadda? The Babe was on what floor, Dadda?* Connie called his father Dadda every chance he got.

"Dadda."

"Pardon, Con?"

He tried to give Shane money, but Shane refused, claiming it was the house whiskey, not to bother, "I won't take it, Con, please now."

The kindness resonated funny. Shane would generally balk at the offer, then finally relent. This time Shane would not waver, and as Connie made his way out of the Blarney Stone into the Saturday-morning sunshine, his mind sparked with sly deduction: *He saw me on television last night, and he won't take money from a guy without a job.*

The game in progress that of a no-big-deal local league, kids from the Chelsea projects and Fulton projects and 49th Street. White and black and Puerto Rican kids, mostly, their team jerseys purchased by neighborhood bar owners.

The Chelsea Rangers vs. Jack Flash.

Desi Burns was real good, Booboo Gibbons was strong, but Arthur stood out. Freddie Patterson was decent. Freddie had brazenly stolen Stan Mikita's helmet from the cargo belly of the Blackhawks' bus, and the helmet's high quality in these rinky-dink games looked ridiculous on Freddie's head.

The only player better than Arthur was Billy Higgins. Billy, from 49th, would make it to the NHL—not bad for a kid from the West Side of 1970s Manhattan. Interesting thematic detail: Billy's father drove the Zamboni that shaved the ice at the Garden. Everybody else, including Arthur, would get sidetracked by alcohol and drugs, the abundance of so much raw talent forcibly benched, bound and gagged by addiction.

Connie leaned against the fence behind home plate and watched his son stickhandle the puck. Arthur looked like he was killing a penalty, but there was no penalty, and as he skated past the bench of the Chelsea Rangers he had words with their coach, Dennis Tobin. Tobin possessed a potbelly and a hangover, and wore dark-tinted glasses round the clock.

A few kids tried to take the puck from Arthur, but it wasn't going to happen. Arthur looked bored, skating in circles, making tiny Kabuki adjustments to the blade of his stick as it touched the roll of electrical tape they called the puck.

"Sky, give it up!" Tobin screamed from the sidelines. "Pass the goddamn puck!" his voice hoarse with an alcoholism all his own.

"Manny!" Connie called.

"Hey, Con!" Manny said.

"What's the score?"

"Tied up!"

The players on the Jack Flash bench were laughing. (There was no bench, there were no boards or ice, the kids skated over the uneven tar of the park's eastern softball field, using some of the yellow-painted lines as demarcations. The goalies stood between two garbage cans and called them nets.)

The long hair of the Jack Flash players flowed out from beneath their helmets. They didn't have an adult coach, they all loved to get high, with some already shooting drugs. The team made Arthur captain for his talent, but also because, at twelve, he was their youngest player, star and mascot both.

"Sky, pass the goddamn puck!" Tobin screamed.

The kids on the Rangers took their sports seriously. They hung out in what people called the white yard, between 428 and 425, as opposed to the black yard, in front of 427.

Arthur had had run-ins with Tobin in the past. Tobin had wanted to hitch his wagon to Arthur in a way that felt like molestation, too eager to appoint himself mentor to Arthur, given what Tobin viewed, based on a comment here or there, as Connie's absence in Arthur's life. But Arthur had rebuked Tobin, and ever since, Tobin played the scorned one. Arthur caught a case of the creeps around the guy. There wasn't anything fishy about him, he just tried too hard to insinuate himself into Arthur's life in some funky way—and even though Arthur felt contempt for Connie, he also knew, for better or worse, he was stuck with the father he had. Besides which, he didn't need somebody leeching on him, and was poised to tell everybody to go to hell anyway—his father, his mother, teachers, cops, movie theater ushers, traffic lights, cab drivers, people on the street, everybody and anybody: *Go to hell with all your shit about what I should and shouldn't do!*

Moments earlier, on the Jack Flash bench, Arthur had taken a strong hit off a joint that, as he continued to commandeer the puck up and down the ice, he realized was probably sprinkled with angel dust. His legs had that rubbery feeling you get with dust. He remembered a story about some kid who had gotten dusted up and jumped in a pool and couldn't find his way back to the water's surface. The kid kept swimming down to the bottom of the pool until he drowned himself, such was the headstrong intensity of his disorientation. Which had not been Arthur's experience with dust. Which made him doubt and dismiss the story as antidrug propaganda. The first time he smoked dust, a few months ago, was with a handful of kids he didn't know in the hallway of some projects uptown. They showed up for a party on hearsay like you do when you're a kid. They stood around and smoked this dust and started to make noises in the stairwell, a kind of chanting, using their mouths and hands, and it went on for an extended period of time; they entered a collective trance state bonded by the dust, their teenage masks giving way to a kind of age-old religious ceremony which huddled them together with their grunts and growls, a primitive music made of hands and mouths. Arthur loved it, inchoately sensing he had tapped a new freedom of consciousness, but even as a twelve-year-old realized the stuff was probably tough on the noggin, and that maybe you shouldn't smoke dust every day, unlike, say, regular herb.

His Jack Flash teammates were cracking up over the fact that nobody could take the puck from him, and the score was tied, and what the hell was he doing?

Dennis Tobin paced the Rangers' bench, but only Arthur and he knew the scornful truth behind Tobin's wrath.

"Not going to tell you again!" Tobin screamed.

Arthur was embarrassing the five Rangers players on the ice at the moment, which wasn't hard. They took themselves so seriously. They looked too put together, yet they had neglected to fully develop their skills, unlike Arthur, who spent untold hours out on this softball field, smacking a puck around, living for it, hiding from his life in the game, straight through sundown into the black of night, until somebody got hit in the face with a stick or something, and only then maybe did you skate on home.

"Don't make me come out there," Tobin called. Arthur rambled from one end of the ice to the other, all five Rangers trying to take the puck. Arthur felt a lock of irritation at his jaw and wondered if the dust was cut with something. He thought of the terror the kid in the pool must have felt, of not being able to find his way to the water's surface, even if the story was propaganda.

"If I have to come after you," Tobin warned.

Arthur stickhandled the puck along the Rangers' bench and told Dennis Tobin to "shut the fuck up," which was, granted, disrespectful, but consistent with Jack Flash's mentality, which on the whole found the Chelsea Rangers to be a humorless bunch of squares and full of themselves. Jack Flash had players who sucked, and they wore funny stuff on their uniforms. One Jack Flash kid wore a World War II fighter pilot's leather helmet instead of a regular hockey helmet. He was Filipino, had a hare-lip, and took zero shit, and he and everybody else on Jack Flash had a ball. Jack Flash brought booze and drugs and music and girls to the games. The Rangers had forgotten, or never knew, how to have a ball.

The Rangers' goalie brought his stick down onto the ice with a frustrated *clack* and yelled at his teammates to get the puck already, come on, get it, as Arthur circled back toward the Rangers' bench and said, "Can't play for shit, none of you," and someone, another adult, reached out an arm to stop Tobin, but he shook it off and stepped onto the ice.

"Artie!" somebody called from Jack Flash's bench to warn of Tobin's approach. Arthur, still in possession of the puck, broke from the group of Rangers and skated toward the goalie on a sudden breakaway, setting him up with the most subtle of moves. Arthur faked left and the goalie went sprawling, hapless, helpless, the sprawling an act of hara-kiri. Arthur, with an easy shot on goal, held onto the puck and skated around the net signified by the garbage cans and headed back the way he came, seeing what he thought he might see: Dennis Tobin moving toward him. Arthur, who had an arsenal of shots at his disposal, nudged the puck up ahead of him and leaned into it, firing a slapshot which caught Tobin in the chest, causing Tobin to embrace himself passionately, doubling over.

"Oof," Tobin said, and just as Arthur went to skate by, Tobin managed to grab him. "All I tried to do for you!" he yelled.

"Hell off me." Arthur tried to wrestle away, but Tobin gripped him by the back of the neck.

The sight of Connie moving toward them induced

laughter from both benches, his rumpled uniform fresh off a night in Penn Station. Arthur saw him and blanched with shame, given Connie's stumblebum qualities, the drunken tilt of the cap on his head as he approached center ice making something of a spectacle.

"Dennis, Dennis," Connie said, just as Dennis hauled back and gave Arthur a genuine punch to his face, which took everybody by surprise, the intensity of it, given Dennis was a grown man and Arthur twelve. Even if Arthur did do something stupid, still, to punch a kid like that.

"Hand on my kid, motherfucker," Connie said, and they started to fight, Connie and Dennis throwing punches in the most amateurish of ways as Arthur rolled away, bent over, face in hands.

"Your fault in the first place, how he's like that," Dennis said, and both of them short-winded after a few seconds of fisticuffs.

Dennis now hurt Connie, bloodying his nose with a wild roundhouse punch, and, sensing vulnerability, moved in to put an end to it, when Connie saw, first, the stick rising, as if sprouting from the top of the other man's head.

Arthur rolled up behind Dennis and with his approach came the terrible apprehension from the people in Chelsea Park that day, as Arthur let his skates glide him toward Dennis, his stick raised like an ax about to split a log. *Artie, no! Artie, Artie, no!* the park cried, just as Dennis turned and Arthur brought the stick down with full force onto his shoulder and you heard the sickening snap, an audible *pop*, and Dennis emitting a groan, dropping to his knees.

"That's it, you're out of this league."

"Fuck this league," Arthur said. He ripped off his jersey, exposing shoulder pads stolen from Paragon which flapped in the wind. He used the tip of his stick to pluck the jersey off the ice and skated over to the Jack Flash bench. Somebody held fire to it, and Arthur took a gratuitous lap, the smoky flame of his jersey hanging from his stick. He skated along the Rangers' bench. "Fuck this league, fuck all you motherfuckers!"

The Rangers cursed back, shook their heads in disgust as Arthur skated off the ice, his jersey disintegrating, and kept on going around the park house, out of sight.

Dennis got up, holding his arm by the elbow, as if already in a sling. "Hell's wrong with that kid. Christ."

But it was all Connie could do to hide the relief which flooded into him. *My son*, Connie thought, *took my back. Yes, he might have retaliated against Tobin in any case, but he did so as Tobin was kicking my ass, so it could be inferred his actions were motivated by a desire to protect his father*, and Connie liked that possibility.

Better still: Arthur had opted for Tobin's shoulder.

Any number of the young sociopaths on Jack Flash would have whipped their sticks down onto the crown of Tobin's head without a second thought, and Connie felt tremendous relief Arthur wasn't one of them. Connie secretly feared his failure as a father would demonstrate itself as a rage in his son potent enough, one way or the other, to incur the loss of life, and this fear assuaged itself with Arthur's choice. A broken collarbone's no picnic, but a straight shot to the skull could very well end in homicide, and Connie rested a little easier knowing his son was not a killer at heart.

* * *

He made a pit stop at the rooming house to clean himself up before heading to the job. Benjamin said Walter wanted to see him right away and that's when Connie knew for sure.

"Not easy for me."

"Don't worry."

"My job's to tell you I have to let you go from this house. Effective immediately." Walter reached into a drawer. "Couple checks, first and last. I don't know, figure it out, case you got something else coming, vacation, sick days, whatever." He handed them to Connie. "Also," Walter said, handing him another envelope, "letter of termination, what's-his-face."

"Grimes," Connie said, naming the managing agent.

"You know I hate it, Con, to fire a man. Last thing, believe me, that I want. Hands are tied," he said, gently touching his wrists together. "Only good thing, I talked to Grimes, got him to let you collect till you find a new spot."

"Thank you, Walter."

Walter's wife appeared with sausage-and-peppers sandwiches, a stack of potato chips on the side.

"Hey, Miss Mezzola," Connie said.

She turned, ruffled Connie's hair with affection, before she disappeared.

Connie and Walter began to eat a last meal together.

"Worried about you, my wife. Straw that broke the back, going on TV like that."

Connie stood before his open locker. He removed the letter of termination from its envelope, the crisp characters of each word snapped out on an IBM Selectric. The management company's stationary stung him, the message containing not one typo: someone had taken obsessive care to make sure he was good and fired. A swelter of loss tried to work its way into him, and he made a quick decision to rip the letter up.

He went to the bank where they cashed his checks. The teller said she saw him on TV last night and chuckled. He picked up a pint at his spot on Lex for old times' sake. He started downtown and thought he noticed people giving him funny looks. Had they all seen him make an ass of himself on TV last night? Was the city revved up for a laugh on his behalf?

Every third thought wave crashing onto his mind carried news of his termination. *You're fired,* the wave said, and a few waves later, *You're fired.* He toyed with a redemption fantasy, seeking out and finding John's Bianchi, single-handedly bringing the mugger to justice, returning the bicycle to John at a press conference during which Connie's reputation is restored and his position of employment at the house is reinstated, but with quiet pride and dignity he turns the offer down, a case of too little, too late.

He cracked open a pint of Bacardi 151 and took a pull from it. Months from now Connie would track back to this moment, somewhere right in here, walking down Lexington Avenue on a quiet-for–New York Saturday afternoon, as the point he slipped into a month-long blackout, finally coming to in Xavier's library, in the middle of an AA meeting at which Justin was qualifying. The following day, June 17, 1974, marking Connie's first day sober. Sitting between David and Susan at the room's outer circle, Justin at the head of a large oak table in the middle of the room. The sound of Connie's tears falling onto the planks of the wooden floor. *Click, click*, went his tears against the floor. The same clothes for a week, his hands filthy, his face unshaven, and no idea why he wept, divorced from himself and still he wept.

Where did he go, what did he do, prior to Xavier's library? Most of it was lost, but some of it remained, fleeting snapshots from the hinterlands of consciousness.

Hand-feeding a seagull pieces of a hot dog on the ferry, the bird hopping toward him on the railing, the spray of salt at Connie's face. Rowing a boat on Staten Island's Clove Lake, a solitary figure, Charlie Chaplin in a doorman's uniform. Taking refuge in a gay bar on West Street called Peter Rabbit, feeling a kinship with the out-cast vibe, the gentle barman offering Connie a hug one morning, some tenderness softening Connie's heart amid his jag. Coming to on his hard-tiled patch of Penn Station floor, looking up into Arthur's angry, distraught face. His head in Susan's lap, weeping in the rooming house, Susan rubbing his back, refusing to drink with him, herself already counting days. Second-acting *A Moon for the Misbegotten*, shaking the hand of Colleen Dewhurst at the Morosco's stage door, her touch soft and firm, her eyes lucid-blue and moist, asking her out for a drink, Miss Dewhurst giving Connie the kindest of rain checks. A drunken ruckus at the unemployment office, only to discover several retroactive payments in his rooming house mailbox. (God watches over drunks and babies.) A woman, Jane, who danced topless at a bar on 24th and Sixth called Billy's, trying to give him a blowjob beneath the tracks of the 7 train on Queens Boulevard, Connie unable to get it up. In Jane's apartment on Morton Street, with Jane and others, nights of self-betrayal, producing dark knots in his character, living against the grain of principle. Susan, David, and Justin shunning him in the rooming house, moving past him in silent prayer. Hiding in movie theaters, the Elgin, the Thalia, hugging his bottle in the dark, watching Jack Lemmon in *Save the Tiger*. Mounting an epic journey uptown to 505 West 132nd. The address of his father's suicide, of Edward's negligent homicide, of beatings administered by Pete Cullen. Two flights up, facing the back. Playing outside as the ambulance pulled up. A man who never gave Connie anything preventing him from going upstairs, giving Connie a quarter to go and buy some Red Hots from the jewboy's on Old Broadway. Connie climbing the back fire escape through the stench of the gas, seeing his father on the kitchen floor in his underwear, against the far wall, as if the oven had expelled him, spit him out, one leg bent behind him in a manner not seen in the living. An unemployed printer at the time of death, having worked in a warehouse down the docks of Chelsea which sixty years later would exhibit the impossible work of Picasso. *Maybe when I'm gone they will let you alone,* read the suicide note. Connie over the course of his life considering the note's meaning, its paranoia, its hope, its heroic angle, which he came to despise. *Maybe through the sacrifice of my noble act,* the note begged, *your future will now be secure*. Thanks to my departure by suicide. Wondering as a child if Pete Cullen had anything to do with his father's death. Wondering if his mother Mary was really his mother. Fearing he was raised by imposters, a man and woman who wore the masks of his parents. The smallness of Edward's coffin, the shaming of the funeral Mass,

the shitty pinch of an ill-fitting suit against his skin. Pete
Cullen's sign of the cross, his sham piety. How terrible
to be the son of a suicide, how awful. Stumbling his way
uptown, only to learn 505 West 132nd no longer existed,
his horror buried over. One more maze of a housing project in its place, 505 West 132nd having been razed, no
such address, and what would he have seen anyway, one
more block of slums, one more shitty-ass tenement, what
was he hoping to get to the bottom of? The emotionally
charged prop that was Pete Cullen's garrison belt. Strap-
ping Connie room to room like nobody's business—or
rather, in fairly methodical fashion, Pete Cullen never
more steady on his feet than when delivering a beating.
His mother's hands around her cup of tea at the kitchen
table, the paralyzed sight of her in competition with the
violence itself for Connie's pain and suffering. The sweating of the bed back in the rooming house, the stain on
the window shade signifying unspeakable horror. Inten-
tionally stumbling into traffic on 23rd Street, getting in
people's faces, hoping to arrange his own manslaughter.
A ringing telephone from a brownstone's front parlor
across the street, thinking the call was for him, letting
him know his number was up and it was time now to reconcile every thought, word, and deed perpetrated against
the good people of this world. *Spic, nigger, faggot, Jew.*
Sneaking in and out of the rooming house, negotiating
backyard fences so *they* wouldn't catch him. Understand-
ing firsthand the *they* of his father's suicide note. Shiv-
ering and shaking in the sweat-drenched bed, wanting
death but they wouldn't let him off the hook, his mind itself the hell on earth they spoke of, and much more never
to be uncovered before the click of tears on wooden floor.

Susan to his left, David to his right, Justin at the head of the table saying, *And frankly, in many respects, I was afforded every advantage, my family having opened every coffer on my behalf,* as Connie, feeling the chilly rumbles of its approach, dehydrated, not a bite in four days, let a brief sensation all would be all right wash over him, before his body with a comical flair of its own poured from the chair onto the floor, where it began to lock and sizzle.

A sober alkie physician, Harold, approached the crowd that circled Connie's possessed form.

"Looks like a grand mal seizure. He'll be all right." Harold went to one knee, loosened Connie's pants, and removed his shoes, Harold all the while calmly puffing on a pipe. "There's a booth, if you make a left at the end of the hall. Will someone call St. Vincent's for an ambulance, please?"

Soon after marking twenty-five years sober, Connie stopped in his tracks on the street by a newsstand headline, causing his mind to cobble together a memory from a long-ago conversation over the cribbage board. John speaking of his time in Greece, where his mother's husband owned an airport's worth of planes. And how a man on staff, Nick, a Vietnam War hero, a Medal of Honor recipient, would take John up in a sweet little single-prop. An ashtray rigged to the instrument panel for Nick's cigars, behind the seats a hanging plant Nick kept watered. John's mother didn't want him going up, he had to sneak over there. *Come on,* Nick would say, *a Sunday stroll in the sky.* The sea a shade of blue you can't find in a paint store. Nick enjoying his cigar, letting the kid fly. *Eye on the horizon, John. Dipping, John, straighten us out.*

Best thing about Greece, John had told Connie. He
mentioned a song Nick loved, and Connie, who loved
the song too, started to belt it out, the fervor of his effort
superseding technique, and with the stairwell's enhanc-
ing reverb he didn't sound half bad. John grinned and
chimed in, following Connie's lead on the lyrics:

On the roof, it's peaceful as can be
And there, the world below can't bother me
Let me tell you now . . .

C HAPTER SIX

HIS WIFE AND CHILDREN CAME TO SEE HIM, gathering loosely in an alcove off the corridor.

Maureen stayed on her feet, smoking.

Balled up knees to chest atop the HVAC window ledge, Arthur stared down at the confluence of 11th Street, Greenwich, and Seventh, lest the intersection disappear.

In a gown and foam slippers, Connie sat strange in a green Naugahyde armchair, his hand keeping gentle contact with the pole of his IV tree.

Conversation next to nil, all of them at a loss—except Steven, who hovered over Connie, combing his father's still-wet hair from a shower, playing the World's Greatest Barber, complete with old-country accent, offering the scene some relief.

"Don't-a you-a worry. I'm-a gonna give-a you a good-a cut. Don't be-a scared."

On their exit Connie thanked them for coming and it was Steven again who broke down crying and reached for his father as an elevator spilled open to the floor.

Those early days a gift, really, the urge lifted altogether, the absence of its calling an almost funny kind of puzzlement. Some tossing and turning, but after a month or two his skin stopped crawling and he began to sleep the night through.

The rooming house and its off-kilter staircase an unsuspected sanctuary.

They talked about everything, he and his new friends, unfolding their secrets and fears before each other, on long walks, across coffee shop tables.

Milling around, waiting for a meeting to start.

Connie's face: an animal trapped suddenly in a cage that is the world.

An older man named Richard grabbed him by the arm. "Don't run off, we're going out after."

Connie laughed—Richard's tone less invitation than instruction.

In the booth of a diner Richard said, "Do you want to save your marriage?"

"I don't know," Connie said.

"Fair enough. In the meantime we get you back into a job. You set up a standing appointment with the kids, a weekend morning breakfast. Regardless who shows up, you'll be there. Let them count on it. You keep the financial support going. Otherwise you leave it alone. You give time time. And you live in the rooms a while."

He took the A train out to Rockaway, plunging into the salt water and surf of his childhood.

He climbed up into a gravel barge down the docks of Chelsea to watch the sun set over the Hudson. Coiled against the river's chill, napping on the sunbaked gravel.

On a borrowed pair of skates he caught himself roll-

ing through the city one late August afternoon, eating
Bing cherries from a paper bag, the scaffolding of a former self seemingly dismantled overnight, a multitude of
interrogations left in its wake.

I am a book unwritten. I am anybody's guess.

"Younger one?" May said.

"Yes," Connie said.

"Good-looking," May said, touching Steven's face.
The boy met her eyes, his nine-year-old consciousness
wide open at the top.

"Tell May what you want," Connie said.

"Can I get a waffle?" Steven said.

"Course you can," May said. "You want some bacon?"

Steven nodded yes, he would like some bacon.

When May walked away Connie said, "How's your
brother?"

"Chump's there." Steven pointed out the window. Connie saw Arthur leaning against a building on the diagonal
corner of 23rd and Eighth. "Looking for money is all."

"Stevie, do me a favor," Connie said, producing some
cash. "Go run give it to him so he doesn't have to wait
around."

"Okay, Pop."

"Careful the cars."

He found a spot working midnights in an art deco house
up on Central Park West. The front car buzzed each
morning at exactly 4:45 a.m. He retrieved a petite, famous choreographer from the penthouse who nodded a
wordless greeting. In the still-dark hour he helped hail a
cab which took her to a studio. And from this brief ha-

bitual interaction Connie thought, *Forget class. It's not about a penthouse. Money cannot buy it.*

That first change of seasons, summer into fall. Being called from a dream to the window of his room by what he thought a storm: there was no storm, just November's fallen leaves, swirling and fighting, chasing each other up and down the block, streaming up and over parked cars, rumbling from sewer to manhole cover and back again, the leaves beneath the streetlamps rendering every known plot—love affairs, screwball comedies, epic war stories. He watched the leaves in timeless wonder on his knees at the window, when he became conscious of himself, felt the quicksilver rush of existence surging through his body, and he was terrified, as if he had never seen a season change.

"I spoke to David," Richard said. "You're qualifying in two weeks."

The row of four windows above Lamston's were covered with a sun-repelling silverish material, each marked with a large block letter: *B—O—W—L.*

"Tell May what you want," Connie said.

"Bacon and eggs," Arthur said.

"Scrambled?" She wouldn't dream of touching this one's face. The hair on him.

"Over easy. And can I get the bacon well done, please?"

"Course you can."

"Also, a small orange juice. And some home fries. And can I get an English muffin instead of the toast?"

With comic exaggeration, May let the pad and pencil drop from her hands onto the table and gave Arthur a look.

He relented with a short laugh. "What?"

"It's the same order I've taken from your father for as long as you're alive!"

Anticipation of the moment had thrown him into panic and suddenly here it was, the scary hour of revelation.

They read a few things to get started, of which he heard not a word.

What he did hear was a very faint, repetitive sound whose source he never identified (but was the cellophane wrapping of the cigarette pack in his breast pocket and how it crinkled with each apprehensive pelt of his heart).

David looked down the large oak table of Xavier's library to offer an introduction, citing briefly with good humor the qualifier's initial, disruptive appearance 147 days earlier.

The room laughed, and applauded, before settling into silence.

"Connie, alcoholic."

They greeted him, gave him back his name, and he started to speak.

The End

Acknowledgments

I am so very grateful to Laurie Loewenstein for her faith in this manuscript.

And Kaylie Jones, for seeing to its publication, with nudges toward the light.

Johnny Temple, too, naturally, and everybody at Akashic and KJB whose efforts brought the book out, including Johanna Ingalls, Aaron Petrovich, Ibrahim Ahmad, Susannah Lawrence, Alice Wertheimer, Renette Zimmerly, Lauren Sharkey, Jennifer Jenkins.

Thank you also: Donald Brandoff, Shereen Brandoff, Andrew Schwartz, James Bosley, Paul Kolsby, Joe Kolias, Steve Shainberg, Curtis Bauer, Jennifer Acker, Brook Wilensky-Lanford, Gary Clark, Bob McIlwaine, Jimmy Gilroy, Michael Little, Amos Poe, Claudia Summers, Jeanne Dorsey, Seth Zvi Rosenfeld, Andrea Callard, Tom Foral, Anne McDermott, Andy Sapora, Michele Remsen, Matt Hoverman, Katie Atcheson, Joe Danisi, Stephanie Cannon, Andrea Cirie, Eric Goss, Liz Carlson, Rachel Casparian, Jason Nuzzo, Val Brown, Michael Mastro, Marcia Lesser, Eugene Buica, Marie-Helene Bertino, Chris Genoversa, Holly Myers, Julie Tesser, Lynn Holst, Steve Dansiger, Marilyn Downey, Matt Keating, Emily Spray, Michael Thomas Holmes, Dylan Lorenz, Regan Wood, Kyle Garner, Heather King, Elisabeth Seldes Annacone, Maud Simmons, Terry Carr, Horace Martin, Hannah Logan, Jim Farmer, Susanne Columbia, Ghana Leigh, Donna Vermeer, Melanie Bishop, Luis Salmon, Edith Schwartz, Andy Epstein, Thomas Anderson, Gosia

Pospiech, Jennifer Neely, Barbara Rick, Joe Barbaccia, Tony Coniff, Marcy Einhorn, Chris Stack, Doug Summers, Richard Lichte, Shannon McMahon Lichte, Jeff Sheehan, Thomas Libetti, Allen Zadoff, Michelle Casillas, Allison Janney, Dion Flynn, Amy Corrigan Flynn, Emmy Gaye, Firedean Schilling, Lindsey Brown, Sharon Lomofsky, Dana Watkins, Rebecca Irizarry, Julia Murphy, Topper Quinn, David Gross, Ned Van Zandt, Shelley Stenhouse, Jerry Mundis, Larry Tompkins, Quincy Long, Elias Colombotos, Anna Marrian, Bill Curran, Alex Figueroa, Martine Bellen, Bob Silverstein, Jimmie James, Neil Chambers, Ylfa Edelstein, Carter Jackson, Kathryn Davis, Eleanor Feldman Barbera, Maureen Burns Shannon, Pamela Lawton, Allison Mackie, Reuben Radding, Tony DiMurro, Eric Zencey, Daniel Reitz, Matthew Carnahan, John Harrington Bland, Patrick McGrath, Michael Howley, Harvey Huddleston, PJ Sosko, Carol Cannon, Larry Vazeos, Jane Elias, Ian Caskey, John Greer, Tom Luckey, Tavia Kowalchuk, Branwynne Kennedy, Hal Strickland, Ricky Buckley, Ingrid Belqaid, Patrick O'Connor, Margaret McMullan, Lily Zauner, Dennis Gagamiros, Lola Scarpitta, Rick Moore, Tessa Borbridge, Dean Imperial, Elliott Green, Margo Katz, Kate Lardner, Wally Johnson, Candace Martin, Allison Lichter, Eric Svendsen, Greg Joseph, Svetlana Kitto, Jess Hale Lombardi, Doug Rossi, Tom Bozell, Paul DeBoy, Andrea Ramirez.

To these people—placeholders in spirit for the countless others—my deep gratitude.

And I want to express heartfelt appreciation for two sustaining communities: the Vermont Studio Center, where portions of the book were written; and Naked Angels' Tuesdays@9, where much of it was read.